'The Shrine Way' illustr   ‿power
of Pilgrimage. As we acc   ‿igrims'
Way, we are not only taken   ‿nester to
Canterbury - with all its joys ɑ   ‿ are also
travelling through layers of histo.   , of both Hindle's
own personal life experiences and ɩ   ‿itual heritage that
formed and inspired this ancient routε.

The book reminds us of the importance of being present in every
stage of the journey – whether we are walking with intention, or
merely living our everyday lives. It encourages us to be open to
the wisdom hidden in the obstacles we encounter, and to embrace
the blessings and beauty of the inner and outer landscapes we are
upheld and shaped by.

Hindle writes that 'walking is the best way of praying I know'
and his search for a greater connection to self through the land,
makes every step a quest for deeper meaning and profound
spiritual healing.

~ Philip Carr-Gomm, Author of 'The Druid Way'

The Shrine Way

An English Pilgrimage

Jim Hindle

Westmarch Books

Published by Westmarch Books, 2023

Printed in the UK by Imprint Digital on recycled paper

ISBN 978-1-3999-6028-1

Cover image from 'Pilgrim Moon' by Rima Staines
www.rimastaines.com   @tilsamka (Instagram)

Map by Luska Mengham
Instagram.com/Luska.illustration

Cover design by Little Seed Design
www.littleseeddesign.com

westmarch.co.uk

Lord, be for us,

a companion on our journey

the guide on our intersections

the strengthening during fatigue

the fortress in danger

the resource on our itinerary

the shadow in our heat

the light in our darkness

the consolation during dejection

and the power of our intention...

from 'Prayer of the Pilgrims'

The Pilgrims' Way

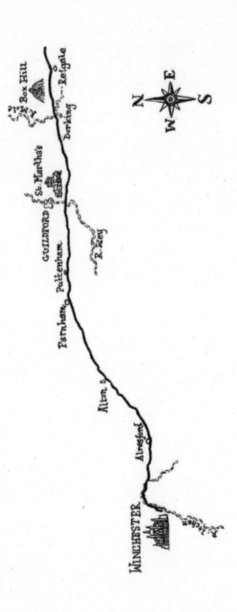

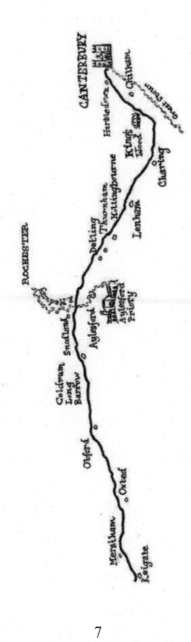

CANTERBURY

Harbledown

Chilham

King's
Wood

Great Stour

Charing

Lenham

Thurnham

Kittingbourne

Detling

ROCHESTER

Snodland

Aylesford

Aylesford
Priory

Coldrum
Long
Barrow

Oxford

Oxted

Merstham

Reigate

7

Introduction

I don't know at what given time I began to think of any walk as some kind of pilgrimage. I'd always walked, driven by the need to reach horizons, by some incessant lust to keep on moving. I loved being out on the hills, to see a little portion of these lands at the only pace that made any sense. But one year I walked down the spine of the Cotswolds, encumbered by way too much gear but still staggering on despite blisters. I'd intended to cut short the walk by a few miles on the last day to head straight to a friend's behind Solsbury Hill. One of my toes was infected and I cooked up the last of my walking stash on my last night out as I looked out from the hills above Bath to a landscape that seemed almost impossibly beautiful. Some little town was lit up in the dusk, the plain rolling on towards a distant Bristol and the sea and somehow it all seemed transcendent, an effect I suppose of a week on the road. But the feeling stayed with me.

On the very last day I walked up another hill in the woods to find two green plastic chairs and a little tupperware container in a wooden box on a stake. Inside, everyone who'd walked this way had written something; Americans used to hiking long trails for whom this was small fry, local girls lamenting the total lack of long distance walkers during the time they'd spent waiting, charity teams, lone wanderers. But all of them were headed to Bath Abbey as their final destination. And I knew then, whatever the state of my feet, that I had to get there myself.

On the last hill above Bath I rested a little in the shade of a shrub by some ornamental ironwork. A passing walker pointed out a nearby hospital for my toe, only half joking. The sun beat down and I was happy in this early June despite exhaustion. When I got to the city, a little bewildered by traffic, the three-storied golden stone of all the Georgian buildings there made my head swim after a week in the hills, as though I'd landed in downtown New York, yokelised by life without buildings, awed by the relative height.

Footsore but full of the buzz of arrival, I made my way (via little stickers on lampposts that seemed to cry out to be noticed, bizzarely, amid every other assault to the senses) to the Abbey itself. I passed under the carving of Jacob's Ladder at the Abbey's entrance, with its surmounting images of Saints Peter and Paul and angels climbing up and down the rungs, then I was in to the hushed, cool interior. I sat beneath the intricate amber vaulting, bathed in fatigue and relief, a little actual pain, tripping slightly from the flood of sensations, the sudden ceasing of a week's worth of walking, elation an actual drug. As an organ recital burst into life, I was nearly in tears. And I knew this was just the beginning.

I formed plans to travel to Santiago de Compostella in Spain, that great shrine of the Iberian Saint, but knew that was still a way off. In the meantime, somehow, somewhere along the way, a seed was sown for another walk closer to home. Had it been the little purple book in the charity shop with the serene-looking picture of stepping stones over a shallow, tree-decked river bed? Or the article in the paper detailing the route and urging fellow pilgrims on? At any rate, my interest grew. The Pilgrims' Way, running from Winchester for some 125 miles along the line of the North Downs to Canterbury. It all became suddenly beguiling. It would be a change of scene from the South Downs at least and topping and tailing a walk in cathedral cities would be no hardship. But more than that I became convinced it would go a long way to sorting out my life, even to somehow make the world a better place. Partly, that was because of that experience of walking to Bath. But above all it was something I knew in my bones. I built it up in my mind as the thing I must do; to start and to finish the thing.

Perhaps most immediately, it entailed a visit to Winchester; the City of Kings, a destination from long years ago, a haven of sorts that I'd first walked to from Newbury, down the Wayfarer's Walk from Beacon Hill and the North Downs, sleeping semi-rough, out in the woods and, on my last night, in a bus shelter in a tiny village, discomforted by neon light and leaving too soon before dawn. That was now decades back. I had been protesting Newbury's bypass for nearly two years at that point but had just left, unsure of anything at all; the trees had been felled, a score of new, largely off-route protest camps had sprung up but I felt as scarred as the landscape itself with all the intimately witnessed loss and I just had to leave, to somehow try and make some better sense of things again. My time there had seen me become mentally ill, scoured by too many drugs and too many evictions, the stresses of campaign living, the minimal food, the mind games of hash heads, surveillance and states of muted conflict. I had been hospitalised for months during the height of the campaigns and again immediately afterwards and would remain on medication for years. In some respects, I was always looking over my shoulder as to whether I would become ill again.

Winchester presented itself as a temporary if unknown destination. I had no idea what to do next or where to go, only knowing that staying on to flay myself by witnessing the by-now-inevitable further destruction was no option at all. On my last day of that walk south from Newbury, I'd passed watermeadows of the Itchen, tranquil-headed and half-starved but not feeling hungry. I talked to a blacksmith by the water who sported a seventies-style beard trimmed at the chin and who wished me well. I knew I was on the right road though I hadn't brought a map and, having discarded my glasses months before, had somehow found my way, myopically, reliant on the little plastic circles that denoted the path, finding them half by guesswork at times, at other times almost mindreading as to just what the sign-poster was thinking at any given juncture.

The city had been kind. I'd arrived right in the middle of their summer festival, the Green decked with stalls and street entertainers, the awnings almost ceremonial attributes on either side of the old flagged path to the red door of the cathedral itself. I stayed around for a while, busked every day and found I made decent money. There were a few Newbury friends and we sat in pub gardens, listless at times with everything that had happened. Some evenings I'd walk down to the old park-up by St Catherine's Hill, a traditional travellers' place and once found a man who was on the road with a horse-drawn cart. We talked by the river about magicians we knew, or respected. The beech mast cast a darkness above us that seemed friendly and alive, lit up by the little fire. My temporary landlady, who kept an open house and who'd let me stay in her lounge without notice, sat on the bed in the van, smoking tobacco through an old-fashioned pipe. I felt out of sorts and quite homely at once. But really it was like home was a long way off still. Home had been torn up before my eyes.

I left later, walking West to another spired city, semi-trampdom, not enough food, making a little money busking, travelled on, looking for refuge, only finding it by the most circuitous events. But that was a long time ago. Still, that early impression of Winchester never really left me; a sense of safety, of something established a long time ago, a foundation I knew nothing of but could sense, like the beer in my belly, the blood in my bones. I knew next to nothing of King Alfred besides the statue at the bottom of the high street and a young archaeologist I'd met who'd said he kept on dreaming of the man during an excavation there. I knew nothing of Wessex or the founding of England, just as I was surprised to dream of Athelstan in a visit to a market town in Oxfordshire years later, where baggy-trousered teenagers were righteous and stoned. All of these things lay in wait.

But I'd passed through plenty of times in subsequent years. The city was the final destination on the South Downs Way, a terminus from the South to other regions and I'd made my way there a few times by then, half mad with hunger or hustled along by fellow walkers but the Cathedral Green was always there, however fleetingly. This time it would be different though. This was to be a more conscious walk than those that had gone before. This was a walk, I felt, that would join up the dots in my life, that represented an embarkation upon and consolidation of strands that defined my whole reason for being.

I was to walk The Pilgrims' Way three times. I could write more about these later walks and other pilgrimages. But that first time defines them all, set the course for what was due to follow. The prospect of Christianity rebounded in my mind; I was seeking to confirm something, to come to a better understanding of my place in the world, to help answer the questions relayed in my mind, full of untamed magnitude, lending a feeling; charged, almost impossible, a kind of elation that might have been actual grace.

I'm Leaving on a Steam Train

I left town in a kind of heady dream. The city was already new before I got there, full of import, full of departure for a new life, a different place but still the same as ever which is to say a kind of Holy Ground, however well-trodden. I felt at home in a way that I hadn't expected. A mob of foreign students thronged around the Butter Cross. A man in a sleeping bag sat playing a concertina in the covered way, slowly and tentatively, making the place feel both provincial and central, as though travellers were coming in from all around, the broad green hills I knew so well covered with the feet of kindred souls. I was aware of Winchester's history in an unspecified way; many of the finer points eluded me but I had a sense of its centrality, antiquity and peace. Its central streets, its hinterland of lanes and greens, waterways and colleges formed a familiar ground; a haven, a hub, an old destination and today a new place of departure. It felt like a good place to start.

It certainly sat at the centre of things. Hilaire Belloc, writing in 'The Old Road' in the early Twentieth Century, comprehensively describes the route I was about to set out on. He highlights the city's proximity to Southampton and the other ports of the Wight, the importance of those ports to the central crossing of the Channel and the access they gave to Salisbury Plain and thereby routes in all directions for the rest of the country. Winchester had been the ancient capital of course, when England was borne out in centuries of struggle against fellow Saxons and the Danes, the incipient kingdom of Wessex finally growing into the country we call

England today.   Alfred in particular was instrumental in Wessex's – and thereby England's - fate.

Winchester, Belloc writes, was:

'possessed of a sanctity which it has not wholly lost.   It preserves, from its very decay, a full suggestion of its limitless age. Its trees, its plan, and the accent of the spoken language in its streets are old. It maintains the irregularities and accretions in building which are, as it were, the outer shell of antiquity in a city... The sacred well of a forgotten heathendom still supports with its roof the choir of Winchester. The memory... is held close in a rigidity of frost which keeps intact the very details of the time in which it died. It was yielding to London before the Twelve Century closed, and is still half barbaric, still Norman in its general note ... It belongs to the snow, to winter, and to the bare trees of the cold wherein the rooks still cry 'Cras! cras!' to whatever lingers in the town'.

Belloc made his pilgrimage at the end of December, seeking to arrive in Canterbury for the anniversary of the martyrdom of Thomas Becket, the sainted victim of Henry II's notorious temper.   Many other pilgrims are meant to have walked the route at this time of year for so many hundreds of years. Even though I was starting in Spring I was following in Belloc's and, as far as I knew, many other pilgrims' footsteps.

I made straight for the cathedral and inside made a bee line for the candles to pray but still took time to gaze in wonder at the vast Norman vaulting, revelled a little in the coolness, the vague but somehow still bustling hush. The cathedral was opened nearly thirty years after the Battle of Hastings and the nave not completed for another thirty years after that. This entailed the demolition of 'Old Minster', the

14

former Anglo-Saxon cathedral on the site. Whatever the lineage, the tale of transition, whatever the gone-but-not-forgotten national trauma the stones still spoke of ancient ambience and peace. Did this have anything to do with the Old Minister stones being used once again in the rebuild?

I was happily oblivious. It was truly a beautiful place, the broad span of cool stone vibrant like the standards and the canopy of any old and well-established wood, despite apparent petrification. In places the faces of carved green men pointed to the survival of older traditions the Catholic Church had incorporated and never entirely subsumed; veins and flowerings enshrined on the sly in the masonry. But I would explore the cathedral in greater depth at other times. For now it was just enough to be there, physically dwarfed but in other respects feeling somehow augmented in myself, my sense of presence and purpose amplified by the grandeur of the columns and vaulting. I left full of a sense of the vibrancy of the place, blinked outside in the sudden sun and very real greenery.

I walked around town for a while after that, trying to find the turning for the footpath I'd need in the morning – The Three Castles Path which the women in the Tourist Office said went to Windsor and would carry me up the Itchen Valley but they couldn't tell me much more than that. This was slightly erroneous advice in that the official path between Winchester and the modern, designated North Downs Way - which follows for the most part the traditional route of the Pilgrims' Way - is in fact the waymarked St Swithin's Way.

Behind the cathedral's presbytery, in the retrochoir, you can see a memorial to the saint. Like many an Anglo-Saxon bishop, canonisation was par for the course and his cult grew from one hundred years after his death in the Ninth Century. Such was his cult's strength that there may have been more pilgrims from Canterbury to his shrine here in Winchester than in the other direction.

Buried outside the west door of Old Minster, claimed by hagiographers to be a sign of his humility, it was said that when his bones were interred against his wishes and moved into the building it apparently rained for forty days and nights, a sure sign of his displeasure to medieval minds, which gives us the modern-day legend as to any rain on his feast day, the 15th July, and the prospects for the ensuing summer. As it goes, burial by the west door was a place of great honour, whatever Swithun might have actually wanted. His relics were moved from Old Minster to their present place with the opening of the Norman cathedral in 1093. It was a symbolic act of the transference of sanctity. When his shrine was swept away at the Reformation it is said monks took his bones and hid them in the precincts of the cathedral.

At the bottom of the high street, not a million miles away from the turning for the Three Castles' Way, down by the river itself, rose the statue of Alfred. The figure before me looked resolute and hopeful, casting an eye past the traffic, past Alfie's the pub, past the chip shop and the café with its very discernable airs, past the neo-gothic grandness of the town hall; he looked beyond all these to some distant horizon that only sculptors or monarchs could see. Was there a hint of a scholarly stare? He had to be forgiven for any sign of fatigue – it can't have always been an easy ride.

One of the few kings given the accolade 'Great', there was no denying his stature. After some early success in the fight against Danish aggression he was forced to resort to guerrilla warfare waged from the Somerset Levels. It was here that, when things were most bleak, he was meant to have famously, preoccupied by his fortunes, 'burnt the cakes'; a probable myth on a par with Victorian notions of his frail piety. Everyone loves a story and this is the one Alfred is chiefly remembered by, which is a shame as his achievements are huge. His arguably most extraordinary act was making a pact with his Danish foe Guthrum after the Danes were decisively beaten at Edington by Alfred's resurgent forces. The pact, where Alfred became Guthrum's Godfather, laid the foundations of the partition of England into areas under English and Danelaw and ensured a hard-won peace for a generation, preventing that which had seemed so certain; the annihilation of the Anglo-Saxon world.

He devoted much of rest of his reign to establishing fortified townships and instigating a new wave of literature and learning. With Mercia, Sussex and other Anglo-Saxon kingdoms subsumed into Wessex's span and with vast tracts of land contained within the effective Danish republic, Alfred and Winchester were the fulcrum around which the country we now know as England was united. The city remained the capital until after the Norman invasion and was not replaced by London in this respect till the ascendency of Henry II; first in the line of Plantagenet kings. Winchester maintains a sense of something older; a time before the conquest's great disaster, a living memory of how things once were that saturates you from the very stones.

+ + +

Armed with the last cache of the day from the fruit seller in the market, I got talking to a man in a tweed jacket who had moved down from London to study agriculture. He was full of enthusiasm for the place and seemed plugged into the essence of the ancient ambience. He wished me well on my walk and it felt like a very good sign.

I then took the route by the river down to St Cath's; my chosen home for the night. The river was tranquil as ever, clear and shallow and full of languid minnows in the reeds. Willows hugged the banks among the already-long grass and seemed to sing of summertime and sleep. That first summer I'd been living here I'd sit by the river whenever I could, the twining current folding the water over itself in a kind of waking dream. I'd draw cartoons, write attempts at poetry, try to piece together something of my former life, grateful for the sanctuary and peace.

As I walked south, a core of lads drank cider from large plastic bottles down by a brick bridge, looked slightly sunburnt, expectant. I was hoping to camp on the traditional site, where I'd talked to the man with the bow-topped wagon so many years before, there beneath the welcoming dark mast of the beeches. But it had been turned into a carpark now and I found myself scrambling up banks to try and find somewhere out of the way to pitch my tent before bowing to the inevitable and walking up the processional-like steps to the hillfort itself.

St Cath's. St Catherine's Hill. I was familiar with the place from various tribal gatherings. It rises up from the city and the intervening meadows and may have once been the original settlement here. An Iron Age fort and later the site of a Twelve Century chapel, its crown is now covered in a clump of mature beeches whose presence lend a graceful sense of sanctity. The trees feel uncommonly alive here and the saying is the place once formed the head of the dragon that the whole South Downs constitutes, for the mythologically minded. In any case the trees, the feel of the place, speak volumes of their own, vibrant and charged; intermediaries. Elephantine fallen trunks hug the ground like recumbent giants and more than just once I have been convinced that figures were sitting on them, only to find it was simply the folds of the dormant grey bark when given a more-than-precursory glance. To walk through the copse and emerge back into the sun and the view of green trees and the hills is to drink a sweet brew.

The place was at the apex of the ridge that once encompassed Twyford Down; the scene of incipient protests against the Tory road-building programme in the Nineties, now tragically marred by the huge cutting for the M3, roaring away far below the little prosthetic footbridge; a painfully thin reminder of the ancient trackways there. I'd been there one winter solstice, sleeping round the fire under a greatcoat as the drums and music whirled around me and again at the tenth anniversary of Yellow Wednesday, when security guards (yellow jacketed) had descended on the protest camps to ensuing scenes of physical assault. That last gathering had stayed in the mind as a new road building programme was just cranking up again at that stage and I left with a clear sense of what I should do next; the encounter was a large part of the inspiration for writing about Newbury and other protests of that time.

Tonight, I gathered some wood for a fire under the beeches, finally getting something going after sunset with the aid of much candlewax. But the wood was all green or just damp and I hadn't gathered enough in any case so that after a while I gave up, scattering twigs in frustration. At that moment I heard a footfall at the edge of the copse. I made my way out, an eye on two silhouetted figures wandering around the outside of the trees. Back at my bivouac by an oak and hawthorn just off the top of the hill, in the halflight, the figures appeared again, a man and a woman, clearly looking for someone, or something. Part of me wondered if they were looking for me, having seen my attempts at firelighting, but they were probably after a dog. Still it somehow added to a sense of something in the air. It felt more than ever a powerful place.

I woke after one, in need of water. My main water bottle was in my rucksack though and the effort of procuring it woke me up to the extent where I didn't sleep the rest of the night. The prospect of the walk ahead was undoubtedly a factor, and the unexpected scramble to find a place to sleep can't have helped. But more than all that, my mind was alive with burgeoning questions, something that setting out on this walk had only brought to the fore. After all these years, was I finally considering myself Christian again, as demonstrated by starting out upon this walk? Attempts at communicating my feelings had only revealed my theological ignorance, had only posed a host of fresh and suddenly newly-urgent questions.

Could I see myself returning to regular Church going? How did I square with the many ethical issues I held with the Church – the clear problems with a celibate priesthood, the preaching against contraception on an already overpopulated planet, the dogma that Christianity, and each brand of it as sure of itself as the others, was the only true creed? More than that though, where did my place in it sit? And how could I reconcile that with my knowledge of the suppression of traditional culture, a sometimes relatively cold-feeling theology that it often seemed had no place for women, a touted goal of purity that at times felt almost sterile, a cure-all clear out like some kind of doctrinal bleach?

I felt I couldn't consider myself officially in 'the fold' until I more formally committed to be so but, even so, could I have ever been anything else? Not least from the fact that my premature birth had seen me receive the Seven Sacraments all in one hit. But the essence of this new and ancient faith, at its best, in how it was meant to be, remained. In which case how could I begin to come to a better understanding of it? How could I best serve it? It felt more

20

urgent than ever that I came to some better resolution to these questions. Pilgrimage I knew was a part of the path for my part. Would completing this one finally deliver the dream I had sensed that time in Bath Abbey? I lay awake, reasoning with myself, full of an untamed rapture with the prospect of the journey ahead, daunted but excited with the lengths I had to go.

I got up just in time to see the sunrise from the copse, a tangerine glow lighting the grass and leaves of the beeches like molten, precious metal. And then I noticed the labyrinth. I'd seen it before but it had had nothing like the sense of mystical allure it carried this morning, the dew decked bright and silver in the light.

St Catherine's Mizmaze, as it is known, is a unicursal (in that it has only one path and you therefore cannot get lost within it) labyrinth based on a medieval design. It is thought it was cut in the Seventeenth Century, the story goes by a pupil from Winchester College sent to spend time on the hillfort as punishment. European labyrinths had something of a heyday from the Twelve to the Fourteenth Centuries, the thinking being they were used as a kind of alternative or addition to more territorially extensive pilgrimages or as a means for meditation. There's not much evidence to suggest this use in medieval times however though this practice seems to have been popular in the Seventeenth Century. The term 'chemin de Jerusalem – 'path to Jerusalem' dates only from the Eighteenth Century in relation to mazes at Reims and Saint-Omer.

Unlike multicursal mazes, originally classical and revived in the Renaissance, labyrinths are not so much a puzzle to be navigated but a potent means and symbol of a consciousness shift. They date back some 4,000 years and the act of walking one, I'd read, can bring a sense of calm, even peace, whereby the repetitions and looping manoeuvres can exert a profound psychological effect and serve as an example of the rewards of not taking apparently easy short cuts.

It seemed rude not to walk it in any case seeing as I was already here. Despite a slight ambivalence as to its effects it still felt somehow initiatory and by the time I finally reached the middle, after several tortuous turns that let me think I'd almost made it before winding out right round the edges again - an allegory for how life can sometimes seem - it had become a satisfying thing, almost in a sense a little hallucinatory. But the sleep deprivation was probably also a factor.

My next port of call was the Cross of St Thomas' Hospital, rising up in the amber sun from the new glow of the reeds by the river. I'd heard wayfarers could get a pilgrims' dole here – a little bread and beer – and was intrigued. But it was still too early in the morning; the old wooden gates, when I got there, were closed, a handful of walkers perplexed by my queries. All the same it was worth the minor detour to see the old amber stone of the buildings rise up, disappear and reappear though the mists and bends in the surrounding water. Another time I'd have more luck and was rewarded with a little beaker of beer from a small white barrel on the porter's desk, along with a tiny square of sliced white bread. The porter told me stories of a charity walk along the Clarendon Way to the city from Salisbury; a full moon, the air full of the calls of foxes and owls, her boots exploding and her carrying on in someone else's. She said it had left such an impression that she didn't want to do it again, she wanted to remember forever the beauty of that single given night.

When I got into town, I drank a coffee on the almost-empty street.   The cobbles and the architecture, the temporary lack of crowds and the general sense of unspoken expectancy made me feel I could have been anywhere in Europe at the dawn of the day.   Though in a not-very-continental fashion I then treated myself to a huge – and hugely expensive – fry up from a very friendly café, where the bombastic and strangely likable proprietor referred to everyone either as 'buddy' or 'my Lord'. Clearly in need of promotion, I only just fitted into the place with my bag.

I left the city at nine, taking a path to the east of the river which a sign said was closed given the recent flooding. But a burry-voiced, middle-aged hiker reading the sign when I arrived said I was probably alright to go on. That had been the winter of the most epic floods in Britain in living memory. Winchester itself had been badly hit and, up the river, there were huge piles of soiled-looking sandbags and big sacks of dumped aggregate, presumably to slow the flow or protect the banks. But, other than a little swampy area by a felled ash, the hiker was proved true and I was hugely relieved to find I was able to get by up the footpath, but equally mournful at the reminders of the recent disaster.

It seemed it had rained half the winter. Large tracts of Somerset had been submerged for weeks. At home, the park resembled paddy fields, pedestrian paths almost impassable, miniature weirs springing up from the ditches in the water meadows. I dreamed of drinking with friends in an old pub, the knowledge rising beneath our feet of the steadily submerging cellar. I watched the river, ordered up a copy of the tide times, signed up to the automated flood alert line, half waited for a call. At night I'd walk down to the waterside, watch the high tide, make silent, inarticulate entreaties. If my dreams had any currency at all, if a walk could in any way help, setting out just as soon as I could held an ever-greater urgency.

Back on the Three Castles Path, under the motorway,

taking the bend in the river, I passed the church and few roofs of Abbott's Worthy; indescript upon the other bank. Meadow walking then the country lanes. Through Easton and then a near-deserted lane that led over a slight rise and past woodland to the lake and house of Avington Park. I felt alright for four hours' sleep despite the beginning of blisters but the combined impact of the large, red-bricked Georgian house, the expanse of almost impossibly blue water and a heat that shimmered a little over the tarmac put me in mind of some kind of mirage. I slogged for another three or four miles; uneventful long roads over fords and watercress beds. Little concrete paths edged the fords. A woman crossed before me over one of these, presumably by force of habit or superstition as the stream here was quite dry.

Skirting Alresford, I was accompanied by an A-road just over a hedge and parallel to the little lane I was on, with the unsettling effect of thinking its traffic was behind me so that I had to keep checking I wasn't about to get run over. Alresford may have deserved more attention and charity from me had it not been for the traction of the path and general fatigue. It had been made the furthest point of navigation on the Itchen by the energetic Bishop Lucy in the time of King John, restoring it after Eleventh Century decay. The place declined again over the years and was burnt to the ground in the Civil War. Julia Cartwright - in her account of the Pilgrims' Way that did much to popularise the route along with Belloc's - described it as 'a clean, bright little town.' Belloc and his companion had been arrested here for 'suspicion of I know not what crime.' On a mission as grand as his - a retracing of the entire route - he was keen not to concern himself with apparent trivialities while writing up minutia of events.

By the time I got to Bishop's Sutton I was tired in my bones. The pub there was closed, which might have been a good thing. Fortunately, I'd filled up on water at the last

24

place. I made my way up to nearby woodland through long fields full of burgeoning green wheat, through scratchy gaps in the hedge past sentinel cottages and overgrown hawthorns where only my stick let me get past.

The woods were a beauty; hectares of coppice beneath graceful oak standards; picture-book models of home. Woodland had long been a kind of home from home for me and this one was grand and archetypal, the understorey of hazel not too dense, the spanning trees above them proportionate and lending a feeling of space. I set up my basher – a lightweight tarp - and proceeded to stretch out under a welcoming trunk in the hope of sleep but ended up just lying there, grateful for the respite. But sleep was not forthcoming. The questions I had started my walk with continued to play on my mind. The imperative of answering them now verged on a kind of crisis. I had a sense of raw revelation: overwrought, like I was an overladen ship, floundering precariously upon the newly open sea.

I barely slept at all. At other times the total loss of sleep had precipitated complete or near mental breakdown. One such time was on the eve of the first day of work on the route of the Bexhill to Hastings bypass, only a couple of years previously. It was the first on-the-ground battle against a resurgent road building programme and activists had flocked from around the country, echoed – it would turn out - by a host of security guards, mostly from the Midlands. It was like old times. Even the security seemed suitably awed and excited. But I could feel the old stress of being on squatted land, of not knowing when and how I might be woken, of not knowing what the next day would bring – ecological carnage or any amount of hectic and hectoring encounters - flipping my switches. There was nothing for it but to listen to an mp3 recording of Juliet Barker's Agincourt. I hung around the next day, joined a posse and played cat and mouse with security guards but I needed to sleep and knew that I couldn't do so there.

Insomnia had become a familiar state over the years. As the amount of herbal sleeping pills steadily crept up, I would often find myself wondering whether I'd sleep at all. Arguably my lifestyle didn't help – literally wired into politics, days and evenings spent online, alone in a sterile, modern flat. However grateful I was just to have the place at all, it was clear that change was in order or that something had to give. I'd often lie awake in the early hours, wondering if this was finally it, if hospitalisation was just round the corner again. I knew it was a long way down. I felt isolated from the rest of humanity, my dreams were tangible and yet at one remove, delivering them felt as urgent as ever, sometimes almost maddeningly so. That night in the woods past Bishop's Sutton I lay awake, waiting for light to bleed back into a certain but nonetheless protracted dawn.

I knew that, however unwilling I was, however frustrating it might be, the prudent thing to do now was head home. After it grew light I walked down little, fully-hedged lanes to a nearby, propitious, country train station and soon I was sat on its old-school platform with a pronounced sense of salvation. Muted cream and brown paint and a general preserved aesthetic that could have spanned any time from the late Eighteen-Hundreds to the 'fifties, helped set the scene. The apparent time warp added to a mild delirium. Only the clear disappointment of the couple in the station-side café echoed my chagrin and I knew that I couldn't explain.

A train arrived soon enough however; a steam train, obviously, and I was being ushered along the greens and golds of the valley, relief outweighing disappointment. The line joined straight onto a modern station a little further down the line where a rapid transition found me speeding home. That night I dreamed of a party with fellow students from the writing course I'd started, in some kind of seafarers' place. My brother was doing it up and it morphed into the family house. There was a sense of general conviviality, reunions with cherished old friends. Angels, although with no obvious wings, were telling me that I'd done well. Somebody gave me a sword.

Returning

I didn't make it back till the Autumn. It had been an eventful summer: things were at a high tide. The writing course had broken up for the season but museum work continued and I was tentatively dipping my toes back into environmental campaigning. The previous summer had seen on-site protests in Balcombe, Sussex, against the first fracking rig in the South East; something I and many others had spent years working towards trying to prevent. It was partly the muted confrontation while trying to stop a lorry bringing in drilling gear, partly a public meeting where the key speaker had gone AWOL at next to no notice - leaving me to help field the gathered crowd in a state of almost complete unpreparedness - that had been stressful enough to make me have to stand back from the campaign altogether. But this really represented the crescendo of stresses that had been building for years. Ever since I'd become involved in the campaign I was more frequently having to double the medication I'd been on for the last decade or so (not brilliant as I was already on the maximum dose) and now, after Balcombe, these gave way to heavy, habit-forming sleeping pills, apparently known for contributing to the development of dementia.

The Breton band I'd formed with friends was going well however and we were playing weddings on a regular basis. I was gigging more often than ever and playing at sessions was a regular event. My home town celebrated the anniversary of Simon de Monfort's rebellion, that early peak of struggle for our rights. Norman-looking soldiers swarmed through the back lanes. College kids set up a temporary village in the water meadows, invited politicians to debates to help mark this seminal point in English democracy.

But, though much in my life was going well and though an easing off from overt politics had done me good, stresses were still mounting like an unseen watertable. The sleeping pills - which the doctors only prescribed with a weary circumspection - were now a regular if not constant part of my life. The gigs were great though increasingly pressurised, a pressure compounded by my pipes being stolen at a festival though recovered, miraculously, when a steward went to investigate a group of teenagers and found the pipes in their various components literally hanging from the bushes in the dark. That was the summer when the situation in Syria, already bad enough, was compounded as Isis stormed through the region. The air was full of potent, muggy storms.

But somehow, despite or even because of all this, the story of the Pilgrims' Way, the intent to see it complete still endured. In a world that suddenly seemed crazier than ever, walking felt like one of the few givens left. If it had ever been anything else, the pilgrimage was now more than something vaguely beneficial; it had become a stark necessity.

I made preparations, forked out for a decent pair of outdoor trousers whose price suggested they hadn't been made in a sweatshop, got all my walking gear packed, got a haircut. Town was full of the new wave of beggars. I bought books on Austerity I couldn't bear to read. I saw a guy I knew, an ex-fireman, who was living in a caravan, eating cold beans as he couldn't afford the gas. A man on a mobility scooter conspicuously stopped to ask me for cash to help pay his electricity bill. I decided to give drinking a miss for the duration of the pilgrimage so as not to make it feel like too much of a holiday.

The night before I was due to set off, I had to double my sleepers and didn't leave the following day, with barely the energy to prop myself up in a café. The effect of the pills on my ability to walk long distance and even the wisdom of doing so if I was to avoid a repeat of the Spring meant that subsequent days morphed into one another and I still hadn't set out. In town a mournful, atonal singer sat on the bridge on the high street. Lads outside pubs grew chopsy. Knowing I had to do something, I headed up to the Ashdown Forest, my already-packed walking stash giving me enough food for five days. I don't know what drew me to the Forest but there was a sense of somewhere so far unexplored, at least by me, and the prospect of vast acreages of woodland to camp in was beguiling; a place on my doorstep that seemed semi-wild. It felt like a good time to see it.

After a ten-mile first day, sitting round a fire on my own in the woods again restored a little equanimity. The Forest, the first time I'd properly walked there, was beautiful with ferns and birches and heather and gorse, orange and silver and purple and gold, expansive and blanketing. It reminded me of other common land from a long time ago; little paths leading randomly to backgarden doors, like foreshortened or suggested fairy tales, footpaths signed like collective, vague ideas, navigation elusive and broad. I hadn't brought quite enough water which made for a slightly anxious night. A ranger on a quad bike skirted my camp in the twilight on a semi-circular track but didn't seem to see me. I felt saved.

The sense of wildness surprised for this part of the country, which was to be somehow matched in the people I came across. A barmaid in an ancient, tiled and timber-framed pub across a little village green greeted me the following early afternoon like a long-lost friend. The few walkers I met were expansive. When I got to the local spa-town in the sun, the hymn 'Jerusalem' came into my mind, unbidden, and I realised I'd had a dream that I'd been there before. By the time I hopped on a bus home, rumbling along through the depths of the counties, I was resolved again to set out on the pilgrimage itself.

As the doctors didn't like prescribing the sleeping pills I could only get hold of a limited amount at any given time, which was beginning to create logistical problems. But having successfully scored a new batch, I was finally on a train a few days later bound for Hampshire. It took me to Alton, which was as far as I could go back to my last point of departure given that the steam train line was now closed for the season. It meant I missed a tract that even Belloc had found tricky to navigate. I spent the rest of the morning negotiating poorly-marked paths through flat fields, stiles aplenty through closely-cut hedges, frequently with little forlorn nails and ghost circles in the wood that marked where wayfaring arrows had once been.

I managed to get lost (but kept on going and found my way regardless), lose my compass (which wasn't exactly called for in any case) and even my trusty length of knotted, measuring-distances string (which was a little more annoying but not exactly tragic). Still, for all this, a man cutting grass by a churchyard seemed surprised and pleasantly amazed to see me pass by with my voluminous rucksack so I felt I was still doing something right. 'Look at that!' he called to his wife, not unkindly. I had a momentary sense of having appeared from another age. Derek Bright, in his recent book on the 'Way, wrote that the route is 'a hidden byway through time... a portal into the country's past' and this seemed a sign he was right. But whatever the historical case, it seemed pilgrims today were now few on the ground.

And that had been part of the appeal; that this was a relatively unwalked path compared, for example, to the Camino Frances to Santiago in Spain. But, also, that it had a long lineage of pilgrims past. At least, that was the story.

It was impossible to walk The Pilgrims' Way and not be aware of Thomas Becket. It wasn't just that the route had largely been formed, or at least had been reinforced by, Henry's pilgrimage in the aftermath of – and in atonement for - the martyrdom. But the very life of Becket, it quickly became apparent upon examination, was much more than just a tale of piety and tragic martyrdom. This was a story of a man who had been raised from relatively meagre beginnings to the peak of political achievement; the chancellorship itself, then the most powerful position next to the king. But he had turned his back on all that when made, against his will, archbishop, eschewing former luxury for a penitent's life.

And yet didn't that make him at times something more than simply a thorn in the side of Henry, who had imposed the position on him so as to have 'his man' in control of the Church? Was there something much more in the story than the falling out, however epic, of two old friends? Was there something in his penitence that was a kind of coda for all that was best, and arguably sometimes worse, about the Christian life; a humility that could also be worthy, denial that could be taken to extremes, a will to greatness cloaked in an apparent self-depreciation that still may have had a genuine currency? It became clear to me at any rate that studying Becket's story would enable a closer study of Christianity itself, would help me answer some of those questions that had been so prominent in my mind in the Spring. For all his drawbacks, was there something there that still couldn't be mocked or negated, that rose above the doubters and naysayers, that spoke of a genuine search for integrity in arduous circumstances, that spoke of a genuine faith?

Becket's remains after his death in December 1170 were immediately attributed with miraculous powers. A woman who bathed in water mixed with drops of his blood was apparently instantly cured of paralysis just days after his murder. Less than a week later a local woman was said to have been cured of blindness with the aid of a bloodstained cloth. He was canonised within an almost unprecedented three years of his martyrdom. His cult quickly spread.

In Toledo Cathedral a chapel was dedicated to him in 1174, as was a church in Salamanca the following year. Other Becket chapels and churches sprung up within years including those at Lyon, Esztergom in Hungary and Catania in Sicily besides those in monasteries at Peterborough and Waltham. Even the newly-rebuilt London Bridge had St-Thomas-on-the-Bridge and he gave his name to St. Thomas's in Southwark or, as it was then, a little downstream, 'The Hospital of St Thomas of Canterbury.' Arbroath Abbey in Scotland was dedicated to him in 1178. Veneration spread from Paris to Poland, his story represented in wallpaintings and altarpieces across the continent.

Pilgrimage to Thomas' shrine began perhaps as early as 1172 and was augmented after Henry's pilgrimage two years later by those keen to follow in their sovereign's footsteps. By 1200 the pilgrimage from Winchester to Canterbury was firmly established. Pilgrims flooded in not just from all over England but from all over Europe for hundreds of years, right up to the Reformation and the subsequent destruction of his shrine. Belloc himself stated there were "hordes of international pilgrims."

But Belloc, Cartwright, the penitent Henry II and of course his friend and victim Becket himself were caught up, it would turn out, in grand mythologies. The great landscape historian Oliver Rackham is famous for the term 'factoid' – a thing which looks, sounds and smells like a fact, has all the hallmarks of a fact but is in actuality anything but. He was largely referring to myths of woodland husbandry in Britain. But his term apparently applies to the Pilgrims' Way as well.

Belloc's, Cartwright's books were popularisations that rode on the back of a high tide of Victorian enthusiasm for the route, for this story of the pilgrimage. Becket's death, his cult and the subsequent popularity of his shrine were not in dispute. And as everyone knows, pilgrims had long set out to see it, as immortalised in Chaucer (though his pilgrims had followed a largely separate route from London). But were there really Belloc's 'hordes' setting out from Winchester?

The first reference to 'The Pilgrims' Way', some said, was a name on a map from the mid 1700's. In the 1920's historians were scornful of the idea that there had ever been such a route at all, as exemplified by C.G. Crump: 'a fond thing grounded upon no uncertain warranty of history, and so intrinsically absurd that it was not worth criticism.' By the 'fifties the Surrey Archaeological Journal refused to consider there had ever been such a route. And Henry – had he even taken this route? And his famous quote: 'who will rid me of this turbulent priest?', the outburst cited as the immediate cause of Becket's murder, that wasn't even what he had said. How much of the roots of this walk were a fiction, an overblown romanticisation, a triumph of myth and wishful thinking?

In a sense it didn't really matter. A pilgrimage was a pilgrimage after all. Any given walk can transform things, simply by walking the land. And setting some kind of intent, as with any meaningful action, formalises this process, augments its effect. In any case I felt sure that people had been walking this way for a long time; it was along an ancient ridge after all, and it seemed likely that not a few had set out from Winchester to Canterbury's shrine. As Bright put it: 'even factoids weren't created in a vacuum and are often simply the product of ordinary people trying to make sense of their own history.' Or, as Rackham had also said: 'aged countrymen, like the rest of us, enjoy a good story and

34

do not always separate what they have read from what they have seen and are tempted to guess at explanations of what they do not know.'

Initially at least, I was walking in ignorance really to all the history. I just felt it was something I should do. My tiny purple guidebook, with its little prayer at every bed-and-breakfasted-end of each chapter was ambivalent about how much the validity of the walk was affected by its historical pedigree. People, it cited, go on pilgrimage for many reasons; to look for their roots, to travel in penitence, or to walk in a quest for healing. A pilgrimage can be a beating of the bounds. Even a homecoming. Above all, to seek a little healing felt as good a reason as anything else. I had every faith in the power of pilgrimage to deliver. One day, I knew, I would walk the Camino de Santiago. Given my health, that was a long shot, for now. But Canterbury? That felt like a thing I could do.

Providence

I negotiated my way across the yawning span of school playing fields, following an almost non-existent path, a gap in laburnum my sole guiding light. The remote roadsides were decked with Tudor-style Victorian mansions and old cottages, white walls alive with the flowering green. Building work and apparent conversions were conspicuous everywhere so that the air was heavy and dusty at once. Towards the end of the day, after an expanse of flat fields beneath pylons, not sure whether or not I had lost the path, I got to 'The Anchor' - a large, grey-walled pub on the edge of a field, Georgian perhaps, as far as the façade went, but low-ceilinged and homely and old on the inside. The barman was non-plussed at best by my choice of drink, depositing the white china of a teapot slightly derisive on the creosoted wooden slats of the outdoor table. Overhead, a steady succession of chinooks and helicopter gunships drummed their way out to the burgeoning front, resounding below the thick clouds, conspicuous in numbers and testament to gravity of the moment.

Becket himself, prior to his life as a religious icon and his ultimate martyrdom was no stranger to war. As Chancellor, he helped lead the charge in Henry's wars of conquest and consolidation. Becket, also Archdeacon, resplendent in helm and hauberk at the head of 700 mounted knights, advancing on Toulouse as Henry sought another prize to add

36

to an empire that stretched from Scotland to the Pyrenees. Almost 15,000 troops assembled in southern France that summer of 1159, kings and nobility flocking from all over Europe to share in Henry's glory. The Toulouse campaign was marked by characteristic brutality with towns, cities, whole regions put to fire and the sword in a scorched earth policy designed to tempt King Louis from his nest in the city of Toulouse itself, his presence ultimately stalemating the incursion as Henry was technically, as Duke of Normandy, Louis' vassal.

Becket had been instrumental in funding the campaign. Becket the fixer, the keeper of state, councillor, confidant, brother-in-arms of the King. As William fitz Stephen, chronicler and contemporary of Becket had it, 'Never in the whole epoch of Christian history were two men more of one mind or better friends.' Toulouse was a kind of high tide, both in Henry's ambitions and the two men's relationship. It had taken some time to get to this point.

Becket, born on St Thomas the Apostle's Day, 1120, within earshot of Cheapside market, to Norman immigrant parents, would spend much of his first twenty-five years in London. His father, a draper's merchant, became one of the four sheriffs of the city. His mother, according to the hagiographers, had a wave of visions on his birth. She was said to have felt the whole of the Thames flowing within her. Soothsayers told her her child would rule over many people. She dreamt of a pilgrimage to Canterbury where her womb grew too large to enter the cathedral. She saw a purple cloth Thomas was wrapped within which magically expanded and contracted. A voice thundered 'the whole of England is smaller than this cloth and cannot contain it.' Thomas later described his parents as 'citizens of London, not by any means the lowest, living without dispute in the midst of their fellow citizens.' After his death he was dubbed 'Light of the Londoners'.

37

As a teenager Becket became friends with the aristocratic Richard l'Aigle, inheritor of the honour of Pevensey in Sussex. It is likely that Becket developed a taste for hawking and hunting at this time and perhaps aspirational ideas, mixing as he suddenly was with important figures of the day. A tradition has it that he fell from his horse into a millstream while riding at Michelham Priory – one of the l'Aigle properties – and was only saved by the miller, who, unaware of Thomas's fall, had stopped the millwheel just in time. The story goes the incident instilled in Thomas a sense of divine providence and sowed the seed of his later religious sensibilities. The priory wasn't established until some hundred years after Becket's birth but it's just possible the mill itself preceded it, which would give the story a chance of actually being true.

Possibly reflecting parental concern over the effects of this lavish and star-studded life or possibly to remove him from the danger of the then-brewing civil war, Thomas was sent to complete his education in Paris just before his nineteenth birthday. Studying arts such as dialectic, rhetoric and philosophy and doubtless enjoying the pleasures of a glamorous city (though to what extent is anyone guess) Thomas was also said to be defensive and a bit of a loner but did make some firm friendships such as that with John of Salisbury who would later prove a trusted friend and go on to chronicle Becket's life.

Two years later he was recalled to London by his mother's death and didn't return as a student to Paris, possibly due to grief, possibly as a result of his father having to withdraw his allowance after the effects of a series of fires on his business. Some accused Becket of loafing, of exhibiting expensive tastes, of pride and vanity. At any rate, his incomplete education, conspicuously his handle on Latin, would return to haunt him. Handsome, charming, possibly lazy, aspiring to a world he could only ever enter as an outsider, it can be imagined why his father was reluctant to fund further studies abroad.

A year later, underachieving, he started work as a clerk for a relative. Some three years down the line, in 1145, quite likely bored of the pace of this role, Becket joined the household of Archbishop Theobald. His intelligence and eloquence were quickly noted, his skills and capabilities facilitating a steady rise in responsibilities. Though Theobald's household was a centre of learning and Thomas had a lot of ground to make up, he was a quick learner and was sent to study further in Bologna and Auxere where he threw himself into his task. Theobald, not easily impressed by his subordinates, said he had never seen greater zeal and fidelity than that shown by his new clerk. Four years later Becket was representing Theobald for the first time in Rome, his success attributed to his oratorical skill. He had become Theobald's right-hand man, his 'first and only councillor.' It was a personal milestone that had set him on course for that summer in Toulouse. That summer and everything after.

Brothers

Picking up the path again I continued into the relative hills, looking for a bed for the night. A pheasant-laden plantation looked promising but was just too strange up close with its serial trees and its serial gaps with their regulated swathes of bare earth. I pressed on and was soon walking down a busy road, continually having to press myself into the verge with the rush-hour traffic until, to my relief, a side road presented itself and, as if forced by centrifugal momentum, I sped down it until I scrambled through a gap in the woodland hedge into an old coppice now full of pine.

I set up my tent and cooked very quietly among the muffling needles. Just a little way away was the bottom of a voluminous garden, a patch of lawn to be glimpsed enticing through the trees like pure, still water. My left little toe, which had played up historically, was doing so again. It had formed a blister while in the Ashdown Forest that had now split, skin coming away like some kind of albino sea creature. It wasn't painful to speak of and I had some little blister plasters but it was still cause for concern. With no chance of a fire, I had a very early night, taking a full quote of sleepers. I dreamed about the war. Possible futures, consequences, stretched out in front of me, charged and top-heavy and urgent. Whatever the answer to that summer's very real predicament, it didn't seem easy or clear.

+   +   +

As Becket advanced up the echelons under Theobald, the country was still suffering contortions as the endgame of Stephen and Matilda's civil war of succession played out. The civil war had dragged on for over a decade and had been characterised by widespread extortion by torture, scorched earth, starvation and an infestation of Flemish mercenaries. Churches and monasteries were looted, clergy evicted. The famous quote from the Anglo-Saxon Chronicle that 'It was as if Christ and his saints were asleep' described the zeitgeist only too well. The general anxiety was reflected in widespread superstitions and heresay; a boy had been crucified in Norwich, his body revealed by a miraculous light in the sky; the throne of England would descend not to Eustace but Henry of Anjou; Christ himself would return to earth disguised as a pilgrim.

Hope for the country rested in an invasion by Henry to oust Stephen. Informed of the archbishop's contacts with the overseas pretender, Stephen put it about that he didn't care if anyone attacked Theobald, who subsequently had to flee an assassination attempt. Twelve knights drew swords and hurried from court to find him, chasing him along the Thames before he escaped them, later leaving the country at Dover. Had Becket been with him? If so, it would have served as a salutatory lesson of what overbearing kings are capable of, not least towards the very head of the Church in the country.

Henry did become King of England of course after fighting for his mother's (Maltilda's) claim to the throne. He had already been recognised as Duke of Normandy by the French Louis VII, a formality that can't have been sweetened when Henry effectively whisked away Louis' former bride Eleanor of Aquitaine almost immediately after their divorce. King Stephen's son Eustace was subsequently persuaded by Louis to join him in an attack on Normandy, a move met with fierce resistance by Henry. Aided by crack

41

Breton mercenaries, Henry forced Eustace to back away and Louis to retreat to Paris in just over six weeks. Emboldened, ascendant, Henry sailed for England in the winter of 1153, braving a winter storm that anyone else would have quailed at.

After a truce of six months, Henry campaigned around the Midlands, capturing castles. When he moved south, Stephen and Eustace laid siege to his planned base at Wallingford in Oxfordshire. A large confrontation looked inevitable but something extraordinary happened; the barons on both sides refused to fight. They largely had lands on both sides of the channel and would likely lose out whatever the outcome of the fight. Stephen and Henry shouted manfully to one another across the river (or politely spoke either side of a stream depending who you listen to) but failed to agree terms.

Henry left to attack Stamford and Nottingham. Eustace parted with his father in disgust, mustered a fresh force in Cambridge and set out for Ipswich, pillaging the Abbey of Bury St Edmunds en route after the monks refused his demand for money and food. He died of a sudden heart attack just a few weeks later, aged twenty-four. Regarded by the chroniclers as a crueller tyrant than his father, his death made the prospect of peace suddenly tangible.

In the ensuing flux, Theobald chose to back Henry. In November 1153, after six months of tortuous negotiations, Stephen met Henry at Winchester. Henry was led through the streets in a grand procession to the king's palace where Stephen announced Henry to be his 'son and heir'. In return, Henry would allow Stephen to reign for the rest of his days. The treaty was sealed at the king's Christmas court in a jubilant London.

As Theobald's righthand man, Becket was rewarded by being made Archdeacon of Canterbury, a prestigious position that put him on a par with bishops and abbots. The following October, Stephen was taken ill with a violent pain in his belly and died hours later from a bloody flux. Henry returned from campaigning in Normandy's borders, in no particular rush, to be crowned in December at Westminster Abbey in a wave of national optimism. He offered stability, assuring a return of the freedoms enjoyed under his grandfather Henry's day and to do away with the 'evil customs' that had sprung up in the intervening time. After so much turmoil, and with Henry's promising start, the population had good grounds to be hopeful for a better era.

Six weeks after Henry's return, Becket was made his chancellor. Overnight, Becket was the king's confidant with the right to attend the king's council whenever there was a meeting. Assuming one of the highest positions in the realm, he would be constantly by the king's side. He was thirty-four. Henry just twenty-one.

+ + +

And so began one of the most celebrated sagas of medieval history. Henry vainglorious, well educated, a lover of hunting and hawking and restlessly chasing across his huge terrains, after deer or conquest or swift retribution. Stocky, auburn-haired, the chroniclers said that he rarely sat down, wearing his court out in the process. Resolutely self-assured, he had no place for shows of ostentation and was frequently indistinguishable from his servants, wearing his riding gear to dine. Handsome, sound-limbed, he seemed borne to be in the saddle, his legs apparently later growing curved from spending so long on a horse. His court was subsequently destined to be peripatetic, drinking vinegarish wine, living in relative squalor. Some said he flew rather than rode on horseback. Louis VII could never really get over his habit of appearing pretty much anywhere at all throughout his domains, unannounced, like a kind of hyperactive Batman. Some called him 'a human chariot, dragging all after him'.

And his prodigious temper – eyes 'shimmering with fire and like lightning' when angry, 'fiery and bloodshot when he was in a frenzy' – could appear within seconds like a sudden storm. His favourite swear words; 'by God's eyes' could rachet up to 'by God's eyes and throat' or even 'by God's eyes and testicles'. Some quoted scripture, said his anger was the harbinger of death. He relied on threats and bullying. His rants were the stuff of legend. He could throw things around amid shouting. Once, famously, when dealing with the constable of Normandy, who had made so bold as to defend someone Henry had just argued with, he

'tore his hat from his head, undid his belt, hurled his cloak and the clothes he was wearing far away from him, tore the silken covering from his bed with his own hand, and began to eat the straw on the floor, as if he were sitting in a ditch.'

And Becket; smooth-tongued, slim, pale-skinned with dark hair. Still fond of hunting and hawking, the richness of his table was renowned and the well-to-do flocked from far and wide to be there. He had fine furnishings and hangings, wore silks, furs. Kept exotic birds, monkeys. His household was second in size only to the king's and, as far as the food went, better kept. Keeping company with aristocracy, he was at pains with every detail of each night. Greeted each guest individually. Haunted some said by inferiority, he felt the need to impress and in doing so performed an important function of state as Henry had such little time for pageantry or even to fully fulfil the very necessary obligations of a host. Henry's meat was inferior, fish four days old, bread gritty, wine sour, beer muddy. Thomas lived to represent the greater glory of the king. Nevertheless his gold and silver

44

plate, the finest wines, the constant bouts of the best-to-be-bought attracted charges of hypocrisy. A plate of eels that cost one hundred pounds.

Their friendship was legendary. Working together, playing together like brothers wherever they were, court or church, hunting, sparring, seemingly knowing one another's minds. 'I know my lord king inside out,' Becket at one stage proclaimed. And then there were Henry's high jinks, his little jokes, borne with affectionate humour by Thomas. The king would frequently appear at Becket's dinner parties by riding unheralded, straight from the hunt, into the chancellor's hall, often blowing a horn before dismounting and vaulting over the tables to take his seat. Becket did his best to be refined. Henry seemed to want to be the opposite; elemental, mud on his boots, he brought the quarry home.

He liked to play games on his courtiers, most famously with the incident of the beggar's cloak, when the two men rode through London on a bitter winter's day. A shivering beggar clad only in rags appeared. 'How poor he is, how frail and thinly clad,' said Henry. 'Wouldn't it be a great act of charity to give him a warm, thick cloak?' he said. 'It would indeed and it behoves you as a king to think and act so,' his chancellor replied. Henry subsequently tried to tear Becket's cloak from him, who struggled to retain it. An unseemly tussle ensued in which both men nearly fell from their horses. When the royal bodyguards made to move in, Becket, clearly gnarled, was forced to back down and allow Henry to take the cloak. The surrounding courtiers roared with laughter. If the King and Becket were in any way on equal terms, it was clear they were terms Henry set.

Faith

I'd been raised Catholic and had gone to mass until I was sixteen, not taken in by, or particularly interested in any theology or sermon but with a feel for the ritual itself. I wondered in the final months and years before I left home how good it would be if churches were more open to the elements, if you could see the sky, the green of trees and hills around you. Eventually I would come to question everything, convince myself that I knew nothing in the hope that any knowledge with some kind of true currency would have some sense of resonance, a ring of truth if you like, if I could only escape my years of conditioning.

It was around this time I got into walking in earnest the South Downs where I lived. With any excuse and often at night I would walk the old tracks, spend time in the hillforts I knew I was lucky to live so close to. I'd sit up in trees on Cissbury Ring while Scottish-looking long-horned cattle grazed beneath me. I'd lie in gaps in the hawthorn scrub on the reserve at the top of the hill and stare at the clouds in the blue summer sky, listening to tapes my girlfriend had made me, with a sense of immersion in everything around me, by night draw cartoons of wanderers and hedges and the hills. Something about the paths and old forts got under my skin so that I found myself reading up on archaeology, was eventually led to works on Druidry and soon felt that a life out of doors was for me. Not very long after, feeling hemmed in by looming academia, keen to play my part in the environmental campaigns sweeping the country, feeling at last there were people out there just like me, I set off for the woods.

I never exactly turned my back on my Christian

upbringing, I just felt more immediately at home with a belief system that first and foremost honoured the earth, that found a place for old legends, for the beliefs of the people that inhabited these lands long before the Romans and the Church that was eventually grafted onto their Empire. And then, a long time later, after I'd been almost physically dragged back to a life in houses - but where I still got out walking as often as I could – I found myself in a place where everything made sense. All the years of awakenings, subsequently buried in returns to apparently normalised amnesia now suddenly were born in waking consciousness.

It clicked in for me on a trip to a city in the Midlands, chasing a girl. We'd met in the aftermath of an epicly failed relationship, a Kiwi girl I'd shared a squat with briefly, her new boyfriend a heroin addict. I'd dream I was carrying her in my arms, emerging from a cathedral like some giant family castle, the coming floods rising up with the current of the hour. When she invited me round for dinner where she was au pairing, still seeing her boyfriend, the sky haemorrhaged into heavy summer rain. I felt like my life had been lifted from its hinges, the fabric of my being split open as from lightning, from mast to root.

The girl from Nottingham had offered a reprieve from the fallout of all this, disarmed as I was by the general warmth of the people up there, the curl of her voice like a kind of sweet hook. I went gathering berries for a seed-collecting project in the Peak District that Autumn, blatting around in my friends' rusty yellow car. They lived out in an old mining village and I'd wander the remnant of Sherwood Forest there, pick out stones that looked like quartz from the paths, seeking consolation, sit by the water of a reclaimed quarry where geese and swans played out spectacular dances of migration and homecoming. One evening, I walked up a hill in the twilight and spawning towns with neon lights spread out in every direction and somehow this was

47

rapturously beautiful. I'd explore further up along the roads and past houses and actual woods that formed the Forest's heart and hinterland. It was all a point of familiarity and fellowship, alive with the prospect of love, its stark necessity, the girl's image rebounding in the landscape as we flew around the lanes until the laden trees and golden green grass of the Peaks in the autumnal sun were made one with the knowledge of her.

But I let opportunities slip, my wounds far too close to the surface. I felt worse than ever, lay in the neighbouring room to hers, barely able to sleep, the shadows of her tomato plants on the window ledge above me somehow macabre, as if they knew my desire and sought to devour me. When the book I'd been reading - a story of a man walking his way home to the woman he loved, the very act of reading it a pilgrimage itself - ended harshly it felt like the end of everything. A storm wreaked havoc in the city centre. The gates to the castle were closed. Flooding erupted all over the land.

But I was buoyed up by expectancy, the knowledge that I knew I couldn't look down and became a regular visitor to the city. I was facing my own annihilation in more ways than one, the danger of the city visceral, background violence constant in the local news, my own destruction closer to my heart. Pain and love coursed through me, like faces of a sharp-edged coin, like I was being shattered and constantly made new. I tried to carry all this with an impression of nonchalance but really I was on a precipice; hollowed and hallowed at once. I'd sit by the waterside, watching the last of the light, the colours of the flaring sky steadily flaying my heart.

That Spring though, years later, I'd arrived at a crossroads on the main high street as the City Hall struck noon, a flock of birds flew overhead in perfect synchronicity and I knew at once what now made final sense; the years of outrunning clouds of external and internal natures all leading to this point; the sun on the street in the heart of the city, the heart of the country in Spring, my own heart now lit up with love. And it wasn't just love for that particular girl: to have and to hold, I could suddenly see, was only one half of the story. It was suddenly much bigger than that, like she was the key that had opened me up. The whole world rang out with the feel in the air, like bells were peeling from every which way and Love I now knew had become grander than all my immediate desires. A friend had a dream on the night I arrived; archaeologists setting right an ancient arch, a sleeper awaking, a knight with a beard, having a pint on the 'Green.

Integrating the full knowledge of that would take years. What had been exercising my mind more recently with the prospect of this particular walk was the ever-growing sense that, acknowledging hundreds of years of an often not particularly brilliant history, there was still great value in a system of worship that, some of the theology aside, first and foremost venerated love and positivity and channelled it into devotion and prayer.

It didn't sit that easily at first. Years as primarily pagan, steeped as much as anyone else in the modern Western world as to cynicism regarding Christianity's flaws, I nonetheless couldn't deny this new knowledge. Perhaps it had been refined and reinforced with something as simple as a candle in a window near a station on an otherwise desultory night when I myself was looking for sanctuary. I had been on the run, unable to find peace wherever I was, feeling the need to keep moving. But that light spoke of faith and a hope in the world I could only quite grasp with my heart. At other times salvation felt like a visceral thing; no intellectualisation, no product of years on your knees but a belt of the will for survival, a pure and raw feeling of being alive, a force that filled up your every cell like the sun.

In a sense it was an inconvenient truth. Like most of my contemporaries, I'd adopted the lazy assumption of viewing anyone talking about Jesus as a cause for alarm bells, that they were suddenly on a par with door-to-door evangelists, looking for excuses for getting a foot across the threshold. But all the same, Christ then was an actual force, a feeling that actually overarched any amount of theology or doctrine, a tangible sense of the light in the world, a feel of redemption that didn't need sermonising or theology. Undertaking this pilgrimage was the best way I knew of honouring that. But I was crawling along half-blind to millennia of theological thinking. It felt urgent I answered my questions, an imperative verging on crisis and the ensuing over-wroughtness of my mind had helped lead to my sleepless state on the hill that earlier night in the Spring. It was clear I'd a long way to go, something only echoed by the very physical miles that still lay before me.

+   +   +

Becket too had had his epiphanies. In 1161 his old mentor Archbishop Theobald died. He had repeatedly tried to recall Becket to his side to discuss his dissatisfaction over a particular tax the chancellor had levied. But Becket, with Henry in Normandy, was not at liberty to leave. Theobald had partly campaigned for Becket's chancellorship as a means of having a Church man at the heart of government. But after Toulouse, Becket's relationship with the king had become more strained and he was browbeaten by the same

50

manipulative strategies Henry used against the rest of his court.

Toulouse infact had represented both the height of the two men's relationship and the beginning of its demise. After the appearance of Louis, Henry summoned a council of war; should he attack the city or wait and see what Louis did? Barons and captains alike counselled caution but Becket accused them of cowardice and was eventually ordered to be quiet by the king. When reinforcements for Louis arrived and Henry called off the siege, returning by stages to Normandy, Becket was entrusted with guarding Cahors. The appointed task was fraught with difficulty, not helped by the king's refusal, as if in spite, to give Becket money to pay his men or buy supplies. Though he fought bravely albeit arguably recklessly, endangering elite troops, the friendship never truly recovered.

On his deathbed, Theobald blamed Becket for not reining in Henry on ecclesiastical matters. He wrote to the archdeacon;

'You have often been recalled and you ought to have returned in answer to a single summons of your father, now old and ill. Indeed it is to be feared that God may punish your tardiness if you shut your ears to the call of obedience, forgetting the benefits you have received and despising your father whom you should have carried on your shoulders in his sickness.'

Becket was not mentioned in Theobald's will, nor, unlike Henry, did he receive a final letter of homily and blessing. The old man died completely estranged from his protégé.

Courtiers were soon placing bets on Theobald's replacement. The odds on Becket were strong. Henry wished him to combine the roles of chancellor and primate, embodying the power of Church and State in one figure, reducing the risk of conflict between the two and placing both under Henry's influence. Despite their minor differences, Becket, Henry thought, was still his man.

Thomas didn't want the archbishopric. He had seen at close hand the nature and burden of the role, witnessing Theobald's struggles with Stephen. Perhaps more pointedly – and presciently - than anything, he must have remembered his journey across the Channel with Theobald, evading Stephen's spies. And he'd subsequently witnessed his former master's cat and mouse game with the then king, including the narrow escape from assassination. Becket also knew Henry better than most, having already served him as chancellor for over seven years. He may well have feared his turning into as much of a tyrant as Stephen ever had been. Becket's friend, John of Salisbury's warning of no man being able to serve two masters must have been ringing in his ears; 'for he will hate the one and love the other.'

+   +   +

When Henry announced Becket's promotion in front of the whole court, Becket had no choice but to accept, even though he'd just told Henry in private he wished to not have it. 'How religious, how saintly is the man you would appoint to that holy see!' he had told Henry, smiling at his own rich clothes.

A deep unease was said to mark the procedure of his election. A rival aspirant to the archbishopric said that Henry 'had wrought a miracle by transforming a warrior and man of the world into an archbishop.' Others questioned how a man 'with the appetite of a wolf', who loved hunting and hawking could be Christ's representative. At his consecration as primate in Canterbury, he dismounted to enter the city on foot like a pilgrim. He subsequently resigned his chancellorship without consulting Henry, claiming he was 'unfit for one office, let alone two'. Henry erupted.

It was possible Becket was reacting to his critics. He was not seen as a spiritual figure and had in fact had to be ordained as a priest the day before his consecration. He was said to be immediately plagued upon entering his new office with a stark sense of his own imperfections, questioning his suitability and qualification for the role. But whatever his motivations he 'put off the old man who is created according to the world and strove to put on the new man who is created according to God.'

He was meant to have stopped his hunting and hawking, put off his silks and furs in favour of monastic garb and, emulating Theobald, began rising with the Christ Church monks for mass at two a.m., then secretly washing poor men's feet before returning to bed until about six. He was said to eat lightly and began to wear a hair shirt and has been portrayed as giving away his finest clothes to the destitute, an ironic echo of the incident with Henry and the beggar on that telling winter's day in London.

Much of this has been subsequently questioned but biographers agree over the vigour of his renewed ecclesiastical studies, 'like a man awakening from a deep sleep' according to his divinity tutor. He quoted scripture constantly in correspondence. Adapting the Sermon on the Mount he declared 'the lighted lantern which lay as if hidden under a bushel has now been placed on a lamp stand, so that it can spread its light far and wide through the house of the Lord.'

But the notion of his Damascene conversion is conspicuously absent from John of Salisbury's earliest account of his life – a letter circulated among Becket's friends shortly after the murder. Some claimed he was a charlatan of superficial belief, driven by pride and ambition. His ultimate conversion however would not so much, or so exclusively, be one of a man enraptured completely in asceticism or devotion or belief. What really changed in him, and would come to define him, what his studies and prayers all pointed towards was his role in defending the Church, on his stance against what he saw as tyranny in any form. It was just that the die was increasingly cast to paint Henry the tyrant at hand.

Many Paths

I dropped down into Farnham the next morning under gun metal skies. It was market day so the high street was swept clear of traffic and parked cars, giving me a sense of how the town looked not so very long ago – and maybe still could in the future. The broad span of the main streets, the Regency veneers of the buildings somehow only added to a feel of a hub in a relative remoteness; an ancient ambience, an unexpected feel of truly being in the country. A little stage had been set up, though musicians were not yet in evidence and stalls of fine, expensive food were already gearing up. Two men were starting early by the stage, making the most of the contents of several silver kegs. I bought breakfast from a little stall; a bacon roll and proper coffee, which felt a kind of spiritual experience after a night in the woods. The whole town was stirring into life before my eyes.

I'd now bid farewell to the valleys of the Itchen and the Wey, the watershed between the two a faint formality in the barely rising gradient it formed. Since I'd started out, I'd been walking in their subtle trough, the tranquil water never far away. The rivers that had marked such a gentle course, that had frequently been punctuated by shallow fords and watercress beds, effectively named the trainline that had borne me away that day in early Spring. Now I stood at other watersheds.

Farnham; both peaceful and charged, was possessed of a sense of wonderful obscurity, like I'd stumbled upon a well-kept secret. Time here was a relative concept. The buildings, the view of burgeoning ridges and woods as I'd come down the hill spoke of other centuries, a sense of being held in a landscape whose signature was stronger, despite being so close to the city, than I'd let myself anticipate.

It marked the end of St Swithun's Way, the days of navigating little fields and convoluted lanes, the string of tiny villages, their beacon-like spires and towers. From here on in the North Downs loomed; not strenuous compared to other ranges of hills but offering clearer going at least. The Downs rolled eastwards and Farnham marked the meeting of several paths. The road from Portsmouth and the Meon joins the Pilgrims' Way just a little earlier at Chawton and Belloc states that travellers going south-west from the Thames Valley or west and north from the Weald were compelled to pass through Farnham if they wished to avoid the ridge of the Surrey Hills. But the major meeting was of the Pilgrims' Way with a much older route.

Once, long before Winchester's birth and subsequent ascendency, people had walked the ridge from the Kent coast to Salisbury Plain; one of the fingers of the hills of the South, radiating out from the Plain's uplifted palm. The portion of the route from Salisbury Plain to Farnham is thought to go back to at least the Bronze Age and became known as 'The Harrow Way', or 'The Hoar Way', 'The Hard' or 'Ancient Way'. Others believe it was dubbed 'The Heargweg', which translates as 'The Shrine Way', forming as it did the route to Stonehenge.

The route may have originated as far away as Marazion in Cornwall and there was a popular tradition, exemplified by Cartwright, that it was used to transport West Country tin. As with other notions, there's no firm evidence of this and the importance of sea trade in prehistory is still often overlooked. All the same, the South East has no source of copper or tin so some of this was likely to be carried overland east of Salisbury Plain. Chert tools from Portland have also been found in Surrey, and the distribution of Iron Age coins as well as other archaeology all point to the evidence of west to east contact along the old route. It could hardly be any other way.

Belloc surmises that, upon Winchester's rise, there once were other shortcuts to the track from the city, heading roughly north. But subsequently the route of the valley via Alton won out, the use of the Harrow Way waned and travellers and traders were funnelled to Farnham, as surely as the chalk hills channelled the waterways. However apparently antiquated they may now seem, these soft vales had become part of one of the main routes from the West to the Straits of Dover.

At the far end of Farnham, over the river and A31, the crossing of the latter hectic enough to both mark a new phase and to rend the moment devoid of any peace or poise, stands a sculpture marking the start of the North Downs Way. The path is one of fifteen trails opened by the Countryside Commission in England and Wales in the wake of World War Two, established under 'The National Parks and Access to the Countryside Act of 1949'.

The act was the culmination of efforts to guarantee the rights of walkers that went back to at least The 1835 Highways Act. While there have always been recognised rights of way in Britain there was a definite uptick in their use in the early Nineteenth Century when the urban masses, inspired by the Romantic poets, began to explore the countryside on holidays and weekends in great numbers. Walking swiftly became a national cult. Railways offered special tickets for ramblers. Tea-rooms and cafes proliferated, local papers featured recommended hikes.

While there were paths in abundance in lowland England, in the North huge areas of land were inaccessible. Idealistic ramblers were spurred by World War One – surely they had a right to walk on the land they'd fought for and for which they'd seen so many comrades die? Thousands attended annual rallies in the Peaks and, as the Thirties began to bite, mass trespasses such as that at Kinder Scout helped set the tone in which the 1949 Act was conceived. The new war only compounded the demand for a more egalitarian country. A committee was appointed by the coalition government in 1941 to see how the needs of industry, agriculture, conservation and access for all could be met. National Parks were also being investigated ever more seriously at this time. As cities in England and Germany burned, designated officials worked away on the shape of a new era for the countryside.

There are of course older echoes too. In Medieval times, pilgrimage was as much a form of great escape as an onerous undertaking. Generally, for the common man, entertainment might notably include public executions and preachers, processions and mystery plays; signs of the power of the State and the Church and the commoners' lot in their wake. Pilgrimage often represented the only real chance for extensive travel in a given lifetime and offered for many an escape for a time from the toil of tilling the land. For many it might have represented one of few means to experience life outside of their immediate locality. They may have felt far from home very rapidly indeed. 'Pilgrim' after all comes from 'peregrinus' and translates as 'foreigner', 'incomer' or 'wanderer', echoing the attitude of many Christians that we are all, when all is told, simply travellers shooting through, our stay on this earth a temporary interlude upon a longer journey.

Pilgrims weren't always venerated wherever they went and a given pilgrimage could constitute a form of punishment; murderers might be forced to wear belts made from their swords. Errant knights might wear chains forged from their armour. Wine may have been prohibited, footware banned. Penitential shirts would have been a signal to religious hostelries to heap on further punishment. As if these weren't bad enough, these criminous wanderers would have to face opprobrium from those less tarnished travelling their road.

And the machinations of the feudal yoke could create criminals as it desired. Labour shortages and vagabondage provoked in 1388 a statute that prohibited travel of servants or labourers outside their home region, their 'Hundred, Rape or Wapentake', including those wishing to go on pilgrimage - unless they had a letter of permission. Fugitive rustics had contributed to the 'wandering class' and those on the road among feudal society's lower ranks could have to prove they weren't peasants out of bonds. In light of the legislation to try and curtail movement, medieval monarchs would often view pilgrimage as an act of defiance. Some pilgrims became lifetime itinerants, beginning one journey as another came to a close. In this latter respect, it's far from an archaic phenomenon.

Farnham was the birthplace of a man who'd also seen changes to the countryside with an impact on the rural classes every bit as great, infact more fundamental, than the reforms of the 1940's, albeit in this case not for the better. In 1830 William Cobbett published 'Rural Rides', detailing his deliberately journalistic wanderings through a Southern England very different from his youth. The open commons had been enclosed, the populations of the villages withering, the cottagers reduced to near starvation due to a portion of wages being paid out of the poor rates under the Speenhamland system. Travelling on horseback, his pace allowed an intimate portrayal of the places and people he met along the way.

Cobbett's prescriptions, in spite of his very political obsessions, were far from any kind of doctrine. He envisaged the re-establishment of the older cottager class as the foundation of a rural order and wrote the very practical 'Cottage Economy' which proved popular among those whose plight he sought to address.

The Agricultural Revolution, or at least that portion of it playing out in Cobbett's era, had a huge influence on his times. The revolution, with its increased production, featured the seismic disenfranchisement of the enclosures and enfeeblement of rural workers. The 1820's represented its lowest ebb, after Cobbett's fondly remembered days of subsistence farming (under the open field system of his youth) but before the more prosperous era of high farming he would not live to see. Though pragmatic and at times a farmer himself (in disposition and sympathy he was never anything else) he railed against the manifestations of the system he saw as so responsible for the common farm worker's lot; statesmen, middlemen, army captains fattening their purses while soldiers starved, utilitarian philanthropists and the cold compassion of their workhouses. He wrote bitterly of labourers living off potatoes while growing wheat and beef for city dwellers. Turnpikes all led to, and were redolent of, the city itself; that 'great Wen' feeding on the body of the South.

His list of grievances went on; stage-coaches, canals, Unitarians, Anglican parsons, bankers, brokers, Jews, Scots, Quakers, William Wilberforce, railways, tea, potatoes. For the establishment of the day he reserved the moniker; THE THING. Self-taught, he distrusted anything he had not witnessed himself and was dismissive of census reports that spoke of sharp population increase, with his experience of the growing evacuation of the land. Nothing unsettled him so much as an unpeopled landscape. Of the census figures

60

returned in 1821, he reckoned that anyone giving them credence would 'believe, literally believe, that the moon is made of green cheese.'

Incendiary, top-heavy at times, his prejudices were counter-balanced with a fierce sense of justice and concern and anger for those who then did not even possess the franchise he fought for. People talk of measuring men in the context of their times. Certainly, Cobbett was self-made, of one kind, stubborn and even perverse in the rigours he put himself and his companions through on the rides. He was suspicious of the dogmatism of the more utopian brands of socialism and yet sought to overturn the order that would allow men to work and starve simultaneously. The list aligned against him in his mind seemed ever growing; reactionary politicians, game-preserving magnates, cotton lords, stock-jobbers, place-seekers. In his eyes, only an overhaul of the political system of the time; 'the rotten boroughs' and the implantation of universal suffrage could amend the situation. He didn't advocate any great levelling, any radical reshaping of the property system, just that each man should be able to enjoy 'the fair fruit of his earnings'.

The downland, weald and valleys he traversed would explode into rebellion after 'Rides was published (though this was not attributed to his book). Fifty years' worth of increased poverty and subjugation of the rural workforce resulted in an eruption of disorder across southern and eastern England. Threshing machines, so redolent of displaced work, were targeted, their introduction being associated with the steady lowering of agricultural wages. 100 were wrecked in East Kent alone. Resentment over tithes for the Church, which administrated the hated Poor Law, were reflected by the destruction of workhouses and tithe barns. Cattle were maimed. Threatening letters, signed by a mythical 'Captain Swing' were sent to wealthy landowners, magistrates and the like. Despite a slogan

61

'Bread or Blood', the riots targeted only property. Their aim? A minimum wage and an end to unemployment in the countryside.

Despite an agreement by farmers to raise wages and reduce tithes and rent, and despite talk of reform in the Commons, the rioters were a threat to the landowners and were harshly punished. 2000 of them were tried in court, 19 were hanged, 644 imprisoned and 481 sent to Australia. Cobbett was charged with seditious libel for articles in the Political Register, including one about the Swing Riots, though his speeches supporting rural workers had also attracted a lot of negative attention. He successfully disputed the case against him and to the mortification of the government the charges were dropped.

Nonetheless, Cobbett was impelled to flee the country twice fearing charges of sedition and was at one point imprisoned for two years for objecting to the flogging of militia men. He was charged with libel three times; not only for his endorsement of the Swing Riots but also in retaliation for his criticism of the Peterloo Massacre. But for all this polemical engagement he remained a lover of the countryside itself and his 'Rides are full of vignettes to the land that to him meant so much.

He was eventually elected as MP for Oldham and he developed a respect for the Northern cities he had once denigrated, not least from the independence he saw in the cutlers of Sheffield. He lived to see the Reform Act of 1832 - the encapsulation of so many of his hopes - and how little it subsequently changed matters. He died near Farnham in 1835, just after being taken out from his deathbed to see the fields he had farmed there the last several years one final time.

There's a twist to Cobbetts' tale of course. Initially hostile, he developed a profound respect for his contemporary, that other great radical and would-be reformer Tom Paine. On returning from exile in America - where of course Paine is a kind of national hero for his role in their revolution – Cobbett took Paine's bones home for burial on his native soil. But he could find no-one interested in paying for a tomb and the bones remained in his house to be passed eventually to a creditor of his son's and so to utter and (so far) enduring obscurity. If we've in any way moved on from the Eleven Hundreds we owe it to men like Cobbett and Paine. We need their thinking today as much as ever.

On The Hog's Back

I walked on down a little lane with whitewashed cottages by the river. A crowd of student types bowled past, in trainers, friendly, but later a little non-plussed when I told them, as gracefully as I could, they were taking a wrong turn. Belloc and his anonymous companion had apparently made part of the way here on the back of a baker's cart and now, faced with the ensuing ridge in the increasing drizzle, I rued the absence of the ride. He referred to this tangentially, as he did to 'the warrior at Farnham' and others, not named, that they met.

I passed through the mixed woodland of Crooksbury Hill, along loamy paths that frequently crossed slightly sunken lanes busy with traffic, at one point down a lane itself to turn by a diminutive golfing clubhouse, carts and caddies rumbling and running over the road then on through a field to skirt round the village of Seale. Some of the pines of Crooksbury had been climbed by Cobbett in his youth to steal, Cartwright tells us, the nests of magpies and crows. To the north, below the ridge, lay the site of his final farm and place of death, the village of Ash. A little to the south can be found the remains of Waverely Abbey. Cobbett worked in the garden of the nearby manor house as a child and gathered fruit for the table of the gentry. Cartwright urges us to remember his love of the countryside rather than the invectives; the steady undertow that enabled - as much as it must have consoled him for – his political passions. He always kept an eye for the beautiful things.

The ridge that separated Waverley from Ash, those very different lodestars of his life, lay before me; the Hog's Back. Sandy soils put me in mind of the man while to my left the

A31, following the route of one of the turnpikes Cobbett so detested, traversed its way along the side of the slope. A line of hills lay to the south, blue and indistinct. Nonetheless there was a feeling of spaciousness, a little wind through towering and isolated pines, a sense of sudden traction. Just as Belloc traced his own pedantic passage, the original Pilgrims' Way followed pretty much my present path, albeit via a little lane, until I got to the village of Puttenham.

'The Good Intent', replete with a monk on the signboard, loomed large upon the village scene, stretched out as the high street was along the road. I drank tea in the garden, exchanging brief pleasantries with the students before their conversation took a turn for the worse and I left them to it. Another time, I would sit in there for hours as 'rain like no other' forecast by old boys at The Anchor proved true. Time stood still for a few hours, a vague feeling of the surreal augmented by compulsory red, felt slippers in place of my boots; a special feature of the establishment. I felt infantilised and blessed in equal measure. Nonetheless I felt on hallowed ground, a sense only reinforced by my passing a woman with a great dane on the hushed wooded street with the number 13 emblazoned on the back of her hooded top. A woman passing the porch of the church as I ate a frugal lunch remarked the place was becoming like the Santiago de Compostella on account of there having been another pilgrim two days before.

Belloc stated that the traveller here is 'in the thick of the memories which are the last to hang round the Old Road... the memories of pilgrims who, after so many thousands of years of its existence, had luckily preserved the use and trace of the way.' A little later he would have a minor fit of precision over the exact route of the way around Puttenham church where pilgrims' counter-intuitive 'leisurely piety' had determined a different path than you might expect and was consequently misleading his research. A pub no longer in existence today was, in his view, miscalled 'The Jolly Farmer'. Was this a reference to 'The Jolly Farmer' of Farnham where Cobbett was born, subsequently renamed after the man, or a surly comment on the mood of the clientele Belloc found within its walls?

His donnish dissection of the route, we should remember, is a reflection of his particular mission to help refound the route long before the days of Atlee and the great gift of the carefully waymarked long-distance paths we have inherited that allow anyone to walk right across the country without barely leaving a bridleway. At Puttenham he was concerned with the route of the Old Road (as he liked to term the Pilgrims' Way) wherever it passed the door of a church; i.e. namely to the south; a habit likely formed in our prehistory in relation to the direction of the sun and doorways to places of worship. Belloc always had a foot in the very distant past. For him his attempt at re-establishment was a kind of devotion to an elemental ascetic that enshrined the primal things. Any given road was 'the humblest and most subtle... the greatest and the most original of the spells which we inherit from the earliest pioneers of our race.'

Over the very different road of the A3 I was almost driven off the path as I began a short and sandy climb into the trees by a man on a large, black horse. Fortunately, there was an artists' studio and café right where he was driving me off to. A gang of goths replete with top hats and black lace were hanging out by a bench outside and I had a distinct sense that the place must be haunted. You could almost taste it in the air; a quality of atmosphere that amounted to invisible company, the very tangible memories of which Belloc had written.

I was beginning to feel a little harangued with the thought of getting clear of Guildford and finding somewhere decent to camp for the night. But, sat inside with a large pot of tea, I realised I could just stop at a little block of woodland a mile or two further on and presently dissolved into a relaxed stupor. The staff were able to supply me with a little length of string I measured and knotted to replace the one I had lost and even my compass turned up, stowed in a recess of my pack. I took in the rest of the gallery at my leisure which included a little potter's shop and a whole exhibition of portraits of local characters and wooded landscapes that echoed my own internal cinema-ed mind's eye.

As I neared the woods up the way a man in his late middle age with a shock of white hair, sat on an antique-looking tractor gave me a quizzical but not unfriendly look as he rounded a corner infront of me. There was no cab, just a curved, iron seat and the thing looked somehow refined in an inexplicable way, purring or chugging away as I passed. I ducked into the woods and camped in loamy soil beneath large beeches, getting an early night.

The next morning, back on the track, the man with the tractor had returned, with reinforcements. A whole field adjoining the path had been given over to what a large banner announced to be 'The North West Surrey Ploughing Competition'. There were tractors of all kinds and ages. The open Nineteen Thirties style with the little iron seats. Tractors with enormous wheels. Ancient tractors with caterpillar tracks on the back of trailers. Tractors that looked like they couldn't go far, propped up by goodwill and welding. It seemed like a display designed to illustrate the evolution of the machines, like something from the Natural History Museum, only with gears and no actual bones.

It was second only to a time while walking in the Welsh Borders where, having just got lost on a hilltop and tenuously re-established a path, a steady roaring began to rise around my ears. It grew louder and louder but I couldn't see the source. There were certainly no roads or rails anywhere near and the sky, as far as I could see, was devoid of planes or, which I had most strongly suspected, any helicopters. Just as the intensity of the noise rose to a pitch which was almost maddening for being so mysterious, the answer came into view as I rounded the crest of the hill. There, thundering up the slope infront of me was a man sat upright on an antiquated tractor. And then another. And then more. Something like twenty prehistoric-looking tractors and their drivers passed me by in close succession, the men atop them sparkling eyed, or else a little sheepish, almost apologetic for having their enthusiasm so visibly rumbled. I was suddenly complicit, a witness to the deed, these men tractoring through the Marches for the love of it, an outing for the mechanical mind.

As I took in that Surrey field over the hedge that morning, farmers and enthusiasts gathered round a burger trailer and though the prospect of coffee and breakfast was tempting, it seemed imprudent to join them if I was to avoid questions as to where exactly I'd just camped with my rucksack and fairly conspicuous tent. I attempted to content myself with two sugary muesli bars and made my admittedly slightly rueful way towards Guildford.

I had planned to make a detour into the town to get some more food and fill up on water but when I dropped down to cross the river Wey, it suddenly seemed an overly circuitous idea and, in any case, there by the path was a little stone grotto with a spring. Engraved into a stone plaque were the words:

'Your upward path, my downward flow

Are made by law divine.

My task is to refresh your soul,

Yours, to discover mine.'

Water provided, other provisions could wait until Dorking. The crossing here at Shalford (probably from 'shallow ford') was once the site of a major fair although, as with so much of the route, its use is full of controversy. The story goes it formed one of a number of fairs along the 'Way frequented by pilgrims. But the dates of the fairs don't stack up with either the anniversary of the martyrdom on 29th December or of the translation of Becket's remains on 7th July. And this theory would have meant pilgrims took a month to walk the route. Nonetheless, Shalford was the site of a major fair up until the Nineteenth Century, as testified by a portrait by Constable.

The theory of the pilgrims' fairs had been espoused by one Ordnance Survey officer, Captain E. Renouard James. James may infact have been the first to revive the notion of the pilgrim route when he marked lengths of pathway as 'the Pilgrim Road' on the first edition 6-inch maps of Surrey and Kent, prepared between 1861 and 1871. In fact the name appeared on maps as early as the Eighteenth Century even if by James' time many people locally were ignorant of the appellation. But he helped demonstrate, as well as catalyse, a growing sentiment of enthusiasm sparked by antiquarians such as Dean Stanley, credited as one of the first Victorian popularists.

James was influenced by Bunyan's 'Pilgrim's Progress' too and drew comparisons between 'The Slough of Despond' (and the Shalford swamp) and 'Vanity Fair' (and Shalford Fair). He thought the topography of much of the story may have been inspired by the route to Canterbury, which, as Derek Bright reminds us, was of course ironic as Bunyan was a nonconformist for whom pilgrimage, with its Catholic emphasis on redemption through worldly acts of devotion, was poles apart from puritanical notions of how salvation may be attained. Those ideas were redolent of a new and more personal relationship with man and God, where intermediaries such as the Saints themselves were no longer needed, part of the justification for the destruction of shrines up and down the land, shrines like those of Becket himself.

Up on the hill before the crossing, can be found the ruins of St Catherine's Chapel, itself a milestone in the story of the 'Way. Ivan Margary, a renowned historian of the Roman era, describes the Pilgrims' Way as one of the most important ancient trackways in Britain, bucking the more modern trend to denigrate the route's credentials. And though he questioned the extent of evidence as to the routes' use by medieval pilgrims, St Catherine's Chapel has a special part to play.

Just visible behind the iron railings that surround the ruin, can be seen grooves in the doors high up where it is believed there was once a gallery. The grooves show that the south door opens in, the north outwards and this is said to indicate the passage of pilgrims' feet. There's not much to see now, just minor differentials in the stonework open to the elements. But it is one of the strongest pieces of evidence that point to a use of the Way in anything like the numbers attributed by once popular tradition.

Belloc ascribed the place with a supernatural importance, sacred as it would have been to a tribe overlooking such an important crossing place. Years after that first crossing of mine, I would stand at the chapel again. Dogs barked, a helicopter could be heard and then seen bearing up the valley, sudden and hectoring. I thought about surveillance in the Newbury years, resisted the temptation to duck under a tree. I thought about crossings in general, the need to conduct them with grace. Belloc and his unnamed companion crossed the river in a stolen boat, using his stick as an oar. It had been too dark and too late for the ferry on that winter's night. On finally reaching the far bank the boat's owner could be heard behind them erupting into verbally violent remonstrations. They pleaded their case. I had lingered a little and made my way rapidly to the awaiting footbridge, stole over its wooden slats, crossed the water, crossed myself, walked over the waiting green to where the track picked up at the end of a road of Victorian houses. The sanctuary of Chantries Wood enclosed me.

Taking the Cross

If anyone is ever in doubt that pilgrims walked the route in any number, they should take a walk up through Chantries Woods to St Martha's Chapel. The path winds ever up for a mile or two with just enough of a gradient so as not to seem too steep and yet drag on you with the attrition of ascent. But what really strikes you as you stride through the ancient beeches, oaks and pines on the still-sandy soil is the feeling of hallowedness, even of company. If this wasn't down to the passage of many feet, both distant and immediate, *something* had been going on here, something that made the atmosphere of the woods ringing and pregnant with presence.

When I finally got to the chapel – square and squat on the hilltop in a little graveyard distinct with box-shaped yews, I was greeted by the garrulous church warden. According to some it was named for St Thomas the Martyr, or after an older name of the place ('Saint's and Martyr's Hill'), although it's dedicated to St Martha. In any case, the chapel takes in views both north and south; the distant blue and familiar line of the South Downs, the Surrey Hills intermediate, lively and green in the sun. The warden proceeded to rant at me about all the houses they wanted to build here – how exactly would the infrastructure cope? The diatribe was perfectly valid of course, though unsweetened by his cup of coffee, goading me. Was it an affront to expect a little hospitality? I fought to recall the pilgrims' maxim I had heard somewhere – 'Expect nothing. Be grateful for everything'.

Inside the chapel, up in the stone vaulting, can be found several pilgrims' crosses, meant to have been made by travellers en route to Canterbury. As with so much else on the route, doubts have been raised as to the crosses' veracity, suggestions being made they could have been masons' or bankers' marks. In Sussex, such crosses are known as crusader marks, for obvious reasons, with extra lines added upon the successful crusaders' return. Poignant then that so many of these have not been embellished with the supplementary notches.

In Becket's, Henry's time, the culture of crusades was in full flight. Henry repeatedly promised to travel to Jerusalem, to 'take the cross' but never actually did. Their time is poised between the hubris and disaster of the Second Crusade – when great French and German armies were defeated by Turks in Asia Minor and an eventual attack on Damascus ended in ignominious retreat – and the Third Crusade in which Henry's son Richard would play so iconic a part. But expeditions of one kind or another were ongoing and to live in such a time was to be steeped in the mythology of journeys to the Holy Land.

Despite the Second Crusade's calamity, the words of Bernard of Clairvaux, who had preached so famously at Vezelay when drumming up support, echoed down the generations and were quoted by Becket's great friend, John of Salisbury. Bernard, no doubt inspired by the successful seizure of Jerusalem in the First Crusade 'used to compare us to punt dwarfs perched on the shoulders of giants. He pointed out that we see more and farther than our predecessors, not because we have keener vision or greater height, but because we are lifted up and bourne aloft on their gigantic stature.'

It's a tribute to the importance of history, rendered ironic by the doomed outcome of the venture Bernard had so passionately espoused; a warning if ever there was one of the dangers of good intentions when coupled to so questionable a cause. The very notion of Holy War has been labelled a colossal oxymoron. And the actual cross adopted by crusaders, given out and stitched to their tabards after the many fervent recruitment rallies and later adopted by some countries as their national uniform; wasn't it the iconic symbol of Christ's refusal to put up any struggle at all in the face of his own immanent death, even stopping his followers from physically protecting him? And hadn't he said when arrested in Gethsemane: 'Put up again thy sword... all they that take the sword shall perish with the sword'?

The Early Church Fathers were clear in their disapproval of violence. But somewhere, somehow, something had obviously shifted. Some blamed the grafting of the Christian Faith onto the Roman Empire and its military mores when Constantine the Great converted after a vision in 312 AD, even though the Byzantine Empire remained peaceful for many centuries. Others, more acutely, point the finger at the theories of St Augustine, writing in the Fourth and Fifth Centuries. His 'Just War' theory claimed conflict was valid if proclaimed by 'legitimate authority', had a 'just cause' such as defence and was undertaken with 'right intention', i.e. with as little bloodshed as possible.

When the First Crusade reared its head in the Eleventh Century, many looked back to and drew inspiration from a golden age of Christian Emperors. The Roman Empire may have lingered in popular consciousness but in the years after its collapse in Western Europe, others came to the fore to strong-arm a little stability amid the turmoil. Men like Alfred. And Charlemagne.

Monks and scholars propagandising Alfred referred to his enemies as pagans while his commanders decorated their swords with Christian motifs and battles were accompanied by prayers and alms. In the Eighth Century Anglo-Saxon epic poem 'The Dream of the Rood', Christ himself was depicted as 'the young warrior' and 'The Lord of Victories', his disciples as a warband, his death on the cross as a battle.

All this speaks of a time when churchmen were compelled or inclined to promote or praise violent men in order to secure protection. In Charlemagne's time and in the Carolingian Empire that was his legacy, public war was seen as 'just' and sanctified by God (as it had been in the Roman times he claimed to revive).

Ecclesiastics fiercely opposed such narratives and combat was still seen as sinful as was later demonstrated by Norman soldiers having to undergo mild penance after Hastings despite fighting under a Papal banner. Abbot Aelfric of Cerne in the Tenth Century wrote that monks were the real 'God's champions in the spiritual battle, who fight with prayers not swords; it is they who are the soldiers of Christ.' Nonetheless, as the Carolingian era faded and European society once more descended into increased violence if not exactly chaos, a militarised Christendom continued.

Religious and secular rulers often came from the same propertied stock. Bishops took up arms and many cruelly violent lords went on pilgrimage and sponsored monasteries. And then in the Ninth Century, Pope John VIII declared that those who died fighting for Christianity were holy martyrs. Religious as well as social kudos was heaped on the warriors' shoulders. Popes offered penitential indulgences for those fighting for Christianity. Finally, by the Eleventh Century, a milestone was crossed whereby actual fighting (as opposed to its purpose) became a penitential act. With the First Crusade, the Church no longer simply gave wars their blessing; it became their very instigator and chief executive. War had become penance, a 'new way of salvation'. In kickstarting the Crusades, Urban II did not sully his hands by dealing with a belligerent social order; he was very much a part of that order already.

The redemption crusade offered to the military classes tended to muddy the waters. Crusade and pilgrimage were separate creatures but they can be seen as different faces, or flipsides, of the same coin. Both involved extensive travel and were conducted for God and the First Crusade had largely been in response to the threats posed to the pilgrimage route to Jerusalem. Urban II actively promulgated the idea of 'armed pilgrimage'. War had become an act of charity, had become transcendent.

Non-combatant pilgrims certainly swelled the numbers of those travelling to the Holy Lands during the wars of the cross, amounting to tens of thousands during the First Crusade, including women and children. They were responding to a recruitment drive that saw preaching up and down the towns and villages of Europe, where the spectacle of the event itself was often more important than the sermons, not least as the crowds were often too big for the preachers' words to be heard. As with other pilgrimages, and as with the armed crusaders, motivations probably included the usual desire for adventure, the chance to break away from feudal bonds, the longing for glory to say nothing of salvation from sin in a society full of the fear of eternal damnation; another product of the preachers' work.

But many were doubtless heading to somewhere other than a temporal city on the Levant. At a time when, with the millennial anniversary of his last lifetime on earth fast approaching, there was a widespread expectation of Christ's imminent return, the air was full of apocalyptic fervour, not helped by extreme weather of floods and droughts. Surely these were the end days, or at least the end of Time? It made sense to seek a New Jerusalem; transcendent and celestial, a city like Heaven on earth.

Amid the common carnage then, amid the atrocities on both sides, the reprisals, the dubious brew of Victorian sentimentality and the subsequent colouring of mindsets near and far, we might spare a thought then for those who set out from churches and chapels like these, full of ideals and high hopes. Of the more than 100,000 who left for the Holy Land in 1096 and over the course of that First Crusade, only 14,000 reached Jerusalem three years later.

+ + +

Out in the sun St Martha's was full of a burgeoning crowd of Sunday walkers. Belloc, here in winter and early in the morning found this place an isolated spot, but reassuringly so, found it held 'a dignity and appeal' he had not hoped to encounter so close to London. He wrote of the hill's earthworks pointing to an older history, how it may have formed a refuge for those from the peaks to the south, the camps and 'stations of war' that surmounted the blue of what he termed defiant hills; Farley Heath, Holmbury and Anstie Bury among others.

With more than one foot in the past as ever, Belloc wrote of how the hill and how other 'such separate heights have called up worship always wherever they were found.' The Middle Ages imbued them with a sanctity reserved for other great hilltop shrines, the St Michaels, the brooding cathedrals of cities in France, Arthur's Seat someway further down the track. 'The Middle Ages gave it what they had inherited, for they revere the past only, they sought in the past their ideals, and hated whatever might destroy the common memory of the soil and the common observances of men.'

We have always been a country in love with our past, even when so much of it is myth. This historiography goes back a long way; Dark Age wanderers were antiquarians too, taking in remains of Roman cities, seeking out inheritance and roots. And in the Middle Ages we revere, people harked back to and were informed by ancient times. The belligerence and blood of the medieval age was underpinned by stories of nobility and grace. Kings and pages alike gorged on romances and sagas of Arthur and Tristan and Troy even as they waged or took part in territorial wars and campaigns of terror and brutality. And yet there was an aspiration for nobility, they were lit up, in their ideals at least, by more than a race to the bottom for cruelty and lust, as some modern takes on the time would have you believe.

The crusades, no less than our modern times, teach that ideals, especially when married to spiritual passions, can be dangerous things. And yet navigating the story of such times cannot be served by black and white dualities, just as crusaders and pilgrims brought trade and interchange, made frequent truces, allied with and bolstered Turkish armies, brought a little Eastern culture home. Time can bring perspective even as, when romance looms, we should not forget the stark realities.

On that fine summer's day, I tried not to think any longer of war, resolved to try and walk a little lighter, to put away the points and counterpoints of argument, to neither cheer or grasp for easy answers. We can all be so quick to reach for admonitions or proscriptions, can be so sure we know the way ahead. The hardest things we like to think we can ameliorate by wishful thinking but hard reality brokers neither excuses or escapism. The bloodshed in the Middle East, whether the millennial invasion of Iraq or its more recent repercussions does not owe anything to ventures from this continent nine centuries ago; its bitter story is a woe borne out only in our recent times. That morning on St Martha's Hill I sought an immediate healing. I sought to step back, to not be a part of the problem, I sought to seek a little peace, to do my best to cultivate that feeling.

Visions for a better world remain a constant for humanity, even if they have been battered at times by stark reality or compromised by cynicism or blind fervour, as if we've lost all sense of history or hope. But life grinds on just as it can soar and we can seek to serve it by the things we know that work. Pilgrimage I knew held just this currency. Sometimes the best we can do is pray for peace and clarity, to begin to make our own gardens and lands a little more Holy. As far as the crusades go, it is said by some that they exerted an unexpected transformation. The lands of crusaders became crusading kingdoms and in doing so a kind of Holy Land themselves. It's clearly a paradoxical notion but can speak for the ideals of so many who sought a New Jerusalem, only perhaps didn't realise it was under their feet all the while.

On Box Hill

I walked down through the sandy soil and pines, found myself thinking of peace, the very real necessity of it. In 'Murder in the Cathedral', T.S. Eliot's classic account of Becket's death, the playwright puts these words in the archbishop's mouth;

"Reflect now, how our Lord Himself spoke of Peace. He said to his disciples, 'Peace I leave with you, my peace I give unto you.' Did he mean peace as we think of it: the kingdom of England at peace with its neighbours, the barons at peace with the King, the householder counting over his peaceful gains, the swept hearth, his best wine for a friend at the table, his wife singing to the children? Those men His disciples knew no such things: they went forth to journey afar, to suffer by land and sea, to know torture, imprisonment, disappointment, to suffer death by martyrdom. What then did He mean? If you ask that, remember then that He said also, 'Not as the world gives, give I unto you.' So then, He gave his disciples peace, but not peace as the world gives."

Right then, that Autumn, peace did not feel an immediate prospect. We were picking up the pieces of a conflict born in the previous decade when George Bush junior 'rode into the dawn upon a tank' as one poet put it. Like many more, I marched against that war, a harrowing manifestation of foreign policy gone wrong. The irony of a president partly fuelled by millennial fervour while orchestrating an invasion nobody sane wanted was not hard to see. And yet the world was lit up by love as the global protests proved.

The day bombers were due to set out with their terrible payload for Baghdad I travelled up to Fairford airbase in Gloucester, a bastion of the American airforce. As we made our way along the M4 in my friend's blue Dodge truck, ahead of a coachload of other protestors, a helicopter gunship shadowed our mini-cavalcade from a distance. We were subsequently pulled over by police onto the hard shoulder, thoroughly searched. When we finally made it to the carpark in the village and parked in a top corner under a tree I realised I'd dreamed of all this, where the carpark was the camp for some medieval army I happened to be part of.

Later, we marched on the base, making our way up through lanes flanked by police and high metal fences. A mobile sound system mounted on the back of a bike snaked its way through the crowd, only for the speaker to be drowned out by a gunship hovering low overhead, pointing its anti-tank gun at the assembled mass of people. We made our way to the gates of the airbase but no one got in. The place crawled with cameras. Even the police looked harassed by events. One danced surreptitiously to the music. As I made my way back to the carpark, I saw a church I realised had been part of my dream. In that dream, a stone-lintelled doorway in a wall by a stained-glass window had led up to a ledge looking out through the glass over a meadow. Hundreds of historically-dressed soldiers were gathered, being swept away by some kind of flood.

I dutifully headed in to the church and there, just as I had dreamed it, was the doorway by the stained glass with the same ornamental top I had seen, albeit bricked up now. Currents in my life were at a strange place, I'd dream of places before I found them in the waking world, déjà vu confirming my tracks with gut feeling. That early Spring day in Fairford, it felt like the world was desperately trying to right itself.

I took a ride around that time to a wooded path below a

quarry on the River Arun at the far end of Sussex. The couple I was in the car with, friends of friends, boomed music of almost unbearable love as we bounded around on the hills at the top of the valley. Life felt rawly beautiful despite or because of the war and the feel of the music was welcome. The path, when we walked it, opened out into raised turf platforms below the cliffs and surrounded by little mounds and hills, covered in bushes and diminutive woods, unlikely and beautiful glades.

The place had been a scene of free parties for years and I'd been to one once – 'Tree Parties' as they were known; a half-drunken walk in the dark that seemed protracted, then dancing and staggering off to a tent. I'd dream about the place years later, trees festooned with coloured flags and more ragged material, branches hung with lanterns, the place alive with music and people. But the parties had taken their toll on the place. Detritus was everywhere – rusting cans, bits of tents, BBQ gear, chairs – things that must have taken considerable effort to get here but were left in the open to rot. The numerous firepits were full of glass shards.

In the dreams there was an inner land lit up; the trees and lamplight formed a hippy archetype of place, full of import and meetings and expectance. I'd dream I was arriving from the sea, following green lanes up from the harbour, following my nose. It was a kind of Summerland where parties were perpetual, or rather were a celebration of what it meant to be out on the land, of what harmony and synthesis could look like.

As we made our way back on that early Spring day, kestrels flew and cried from one of the cliffs and I had a sudden feel of homecoming, a feel for the potential of the place, a call that it needed to be cared for. I subsequently organised a cleaning contingent, formed from willing friends, got numbers for local rangers to organise rubbish collection, bought rubble sacks and gloves, borrowed barrows, spades. I decided to make the Easter weekend the one to go for – a camping, cleaning party whose potential and scale grew in my mind as I contemplated it. Our globe-trotting neighbours would bring a tepee. It would be a coming back to the land, a kind of triumphant arrival, an antidote to everything else that was happening.

After the 'liberation' of Baghdad, I watched on a tiny TV, disbelieving, as Sadham Hussein's statue was toppled in a fit of public theatre. I was more than half mad after reading the papers, saved up at my parents', not least the story of the boy who'd lost his arms. Later, when the boy was freshly patriated in the UK and at an event, Tony Blair would try to shake his hand.

That week, the city had become a bright beacon in the early April sun. The offices of the local alternative news sheet I had some reason to visit, up at the end of one of the ubiquitous regency terraced streets and across a park, up a hill, became the very centre of the city, the rooms a kind of inner keep within a sacred citadel. I went to the local centre for the unemployed, (or simply the 'Ployed' as friends termed it) and had a semi-argument with a woman high as a kite who was on about the Rapture – that apparent ascension to Heaven of the worthy. I was a great believer in Paradise on Earth. Like the offices, the 'Ployed was high on a hill, its café three or four stories up and the city was laid out below us in the sun, full of an unspoken promise. Rivulets of little, white-walled terraced Victorian houses decked the ridges, bright with the light, the sea a clear aquamarine. This, it felt, was as high as you could possible go. Some kind of full-on mystic sat nearby - heavy set, auburn beard twining in plaits - was under the impression I was Jesus. Given it was the day before Good Friday, this did little for my peace of mind.

Friends were due round for dinner that evening but I was too far gone to cook. Somewhat shocked, they bought chips and we sat in the garden, drinking wine – a bottle of

'Southern Star' - and I mused again on the recent revelation I'd heard that New Zealand had been discovered by an expedition sent to enquire as to what Venus looked like in the Southern Hemisphere. The garden felt heavy, enchanted, and I suddenly wished I had got some firecrackers as the mystic in the 'Ployed had suggested. Nonetheless things were lit up, the chestnut tree there in full leaf and as beautiful as ever, the windows of the three-storied, terraced housing all around shining for the Holy Festival.

I'd dream of the 'Ployed another time, an oak tree outside, golden-leaved, somehow forming a bridge into a higher window. Like the lights in the houses around us in the garden that night, the building was alive with bright colour, the walls made of flint. There was a sense of arrival, of a kind of college or bastion. Dreams at that time were full of the city in summer, banners hanging from the balconies and windows so that somehow I was also in Spain, hosts of black-haired women looking out from above as I made my way through, eventually finding a harbour again, the sea becalmed and beguiling at once with a sense of gentle but potent potential, the water as clear as the dawn.

I woke early that Good Friday and, strident, walked down the London Road with the holiday traffic and early heat. Without any water, I somehow found a place where I could buy a loaf of bread, sat by the steps to a grand though slightly dishevelled branchline station while a woman with crutches and only one leg made her way up the side street towards me, the rubber and metal clacking on the paving tiles. It was as if she spoke of the suffering of the world, laying it firmly upon me. I found myself weeping.

It took me the rest of the day to pack my bag, sleep deprivation and confusion dulling my actions and movements like some kind of bad dream. Finally, as it grew dark, I strapped a little candle lantern to the back of my bag and set off for the dishevelled station up the avenue of an elm-lined street. The last train had been an escape. I made my way in the dark along a familiar route to the family home while a mob from closing time howled behind me. I hid in a church yard and crossed the river over an old wooden bridge and, finally at home, spent half the night resurrecting a candle whose wick had been half buried in wax.

I sat in my room the next morning, curtains drawn, screensaver on of the bottom of the sea, as if this would help me to hide from George Bush. My sister, I was convinced the next morning, was some kind of elf. The whole house was Tolkienesque. A van load of friends turned up to go to the camp by the river but one friend, who my family let up to my room, sat blocking the light, clawed at my arm in apparent affection as I lay on the bed and I could only turn away. My sister had to tell her, in tears now, about my condition, banished for so long. I was put on a medication I thought I had seen the back of years before. My father put up a Victorian painting of a wounded Napoleonic soldier being borne away, his comrades all rallying round. Three doves appeared to nestle in the eaves, carrying little branches for new nests.

+   +   +

In many ways, it was a bleak intermission, not least as it heralded a return to life on medication for me. Even the knowledge of war had taken its toll. But still, I felt lit up with the apparently unlikely promise in the air. However bleak the news may be, there is always a counterforce there if we are willing to see it. Sometimes it can be transcendent, at others adherence to it can feel bloodyminded, a thing we have to strive for. But peace in the world, even at an hour like this; how could I best amplify it, seek to serve it? Did I even know what it meant? I was only full of sensations that were beyond an understanding solely of the mind, as simple and strong as the newborn young sun at the return of the Summer.

An often-abused quote of Jesus runs like this: "Don't imagine that I came to bring peace to the earth! No, rather, a sword. I have come to set a man against his father, and a daughter against her mother, and a daughter-in-law against her mother-in-law – a man's worst enemies will be found right in his own home! If you love your father and mother more than you love me, you are not worthy of being mine; or if you love your son or daughter more than me, you are not worthy of being mine."

It's contentious stuff. While it has been taken frequently to justify the use of force, the warfare spoken of here is spiritual not physical, the sword one which cuts away at untruth. For the poet Philip Britts, peace is "the weaponry of love and redemption... not carnal weaponry, but the weaponry of the will to Truth." Its war is not a physical battlefield but that of "the creator against the destroyer; the war of the will to life against the will to death; the war of love against hate, of unity against separation." In his popular book 'Seeking Peace', Johann Christolph Arnold writes "we cannot wait for heaven, for God's reign of peace, to fall into our laps. We must go after it zealously." The very word *jihad* is as much about this internal spiritual battle, this striving, than any other kind of holy war.

Peace then comes in different forms, or perhaps in ways that override simplistic definitions. Arnold quotes Rabbi Kenneth L. Cohen: "Darkness is the absence of light, but peace is not just the cessation of hostilities. Treaties may be signed, ambassadors exchanged, and armies sent home, yet there still may not be peace. Peace is metaphysical and cosmic in its implications. It is more than the absence of war. Peace, in fact, is not the absence of anything, but rather the ultimate affirmation of what can be."

That Spring in the Midlands when the city and the people had spoken so clear to my heart I'd had other epiphanies. The Midlands and the North had been unchartered territory for a while and the impression of the cities up there was initially a little unsettling; the scale of them and their being so relatively close to one another, the amount of people there. It brought home a sense of the vastness of humanity in the country in a way that London somehow never had. And districts of the city were poorer, rougher, the centre streets heavily pocketed with desperate beggars who got in your face. I'd dream of the social centre my friends had set up there, huge with subterranean rooms and the prospect of something that felt both benevolent and genuinely revolutionary. "Another World is Possible" said their posters.

The wars in Iraq and Afghanistan were still in full flight. I was on a low dose of meds - arguably not enough and I was stringing out my prescriptions from mortification of having to take them at all. Nonetheless, I came bearing gifts of candles and incense. We played a session where I drank enough to see the colours the tunes made in my mind. It was all so full of promise. Things were lit up. I'd been reading of Sufis and Rumi, played with the feeling of beautiful fire of the spirit as if I was sculpting or writing the book of my heart. A man in a pub the next day slept sitting upright, his face resting dignified, propped up by his elbow on the bar. His pint was full, awaiting him, and this was like Jerusalem.

But sleep for me proved elusive. I left my friends' house in the city centre early one morning, keen to avoid detection, and took a bus to the mining village, hid for a while in the woods. Nonetheless, Asian shopkeepers spoke of the Promised Land and I could actually see it – the feeling of how things were meant to be; an Island, a World here at last woken up, a dream that I knew could come true, the machinations of the enemy belittled and predictable, something that our shared humanity could conquer. As I waited on the platform for the train home a man seemed to recognise me, shook my hand, then shook the hands of everyone else on the crowded platform wishing "Peace be with you" to everyone he met.

On the way home, by which point I hadn't slept for days, a kindly old woman sitting opposite me babbled pleasant irrelevancies for what seemed like hours to keep me in a good place. But when I looked up at her as I left there was nobody there. When I finally got home, my new housemate was manically sanding his shelves, making the place uninhabitable again, and I made my way to a pub across town en route to somewhere more closely resembling sanctuary. The next day, they painted a knight on the board outside with a pint like the Grail. "At last, I have found it!" it read.

+   +   +

Back that Autumn on pilgrimage, just past St Martha's, I walked past a carpark and on to a country lane overhung with a deep summer mast and punctuated by a ford with a little platform for those on foot. Then a path perpendicularly upwards along the line of a little woodland so that I was back on top of the North Downs. Presently I came to a beauty spot, rammed full of bikers and day trippers, some sat in their cars still looking out over the Weald as if they were pensioners by the sea, families crammed in queues around the brown brick of the serving area like wasps round a jar of old fruit. I wasn't above them; a coffee and an egg and bacon roll induced a feeling of euphoria after my two miniscule muesli bars hours earlier.

Over an A-road I headed into the trees. The woods; those of Hackhurst and the White Downs, would be my companion for much of the rest of the day, along with the knots of Sunday walkers I would pass every couple of hundred of yards. The trees were mostly a mix of beeches and yew, with beautiful maiden trees here and there grown out from once ubiquitous hedges, remnants from a time when large parts of the Downs were enclosed, the remaining woodland having needed to be fenced off from sheep along the intersecting drove roads. Much of that which survives is ancient woodland but secondary woodland - i.e. that planted up or simply allowed to grow since the early 1600's – is a common feature too.

Pockets of open grassland remain and it is easy to imagine a time when sheep pasture here was as common a phenomenon as that which we associate with the South Downs, beckoning over the Weald, or for that matter downland further West. W. H. Hudson, writing in 'A Shepherd's Life', recounts a little of the effect of the animals on the Wiltshire downland habitat;

'Where the sheep are taken away the turf loses the smooth, elastic character which makes it better to walk on than the most perfect lawn. The sheep fed closely and everything that grew on the down – grasses, clovers, and numerous small creeping herbs – had acquired the habitat of growing and flowering close to the ground, every species and every individual plant striving, with the unconscious intelligence that is in all growing things, to hide its leaves and pushing sprays under the others, to escape the nibbling teeth...'

My pack felt especially heavy and I was aware that I needed to cover some ground. I stopped for a while where the path took a sharp left, uphill past beeches more beautiful than any I remembered, a feel in the air of something untouched by walkers or towns, one of those spots you at times come across that ask you to linger for reasons you can never describe but which are as undeniable as earth or the air when you find them. World War Two pill boxes cropped up along the track fairly frequently here; bat roosts now but once a second line of defence in the event of invasion. Some put the feeling here amid these trees as tokens of the Canadians who doubtless whiled away the hours and years before the ill-fated Normandy landings or a distant D-Day. A kindly couple looked at me curiously as I struggled to regain a little poise after the weight of my pack and said that they hoped I was enjoying the walk, as if in an unspoken plea to enjoy this place of peace before hurrying on, just as the Canadians may have wanted to stay here forever.

Optimistic, I'd fixed my intention on the distant Box Hill; here and there beckoning through gaps in the trees, standing out shouldering, simultaneously soft and as solid as any other downland beacon, other hilltops staggering out before the eye at every vantage point. As Belloc had put it; 'It stood out like a cape along our coasting journey, our navigation of the line of the Downs.' The map showed a pub there where I was sure I could eat before melting away to set up my camp in the hill's hinterland of woods. But time was getting on, there was a church on the map – whose yard, I hoped, might provide my water for the night - making stopping two or three miles from the hill suddenly feasible. It would have the advantage too of my being able to drop down into Dorking the following morning to pick up some much-needed supplies.

Dorking presented itself through the gaps here and there surprisingly inviting. A tall church spire rose from the town

– its chief visible feature from here – amid a blur of red roofing and the surrounding very voluminous green of the Weald. It held a sense of unexpected modesty of scale which countered the visions of the place my preconceptions had conjured up, its proportions like that of some medieval citadel, without the walls, a vision of a perfect town, like some earthly manifestation of a heavenly ideal of man's place within nature.

I didn't know if the reality would match when up close. Belloc certainly did not spare his words, even though he didn't mention Dorking, or any other town, by name. After describing the Downs on which I now walked he'd stated; 'At the end of a day's work, a short winter day's, it was possible to separate this noble mark of what was once a true county of Surrey; to separate it even in the mind from the taint of our time and the decay and vileness which hang like a smell of evil over whatever has suffered the influence of our great towns.' Perhaps he was referring to that which lay closer to London, no less then than now, threatening the wider area, the trees of the Weald over which I now could look so lovingly, the prospective rash of new builds highlighted by the caretaker on St Martha's.

In a world of at times conflicting pressures, figures like Belloc speak for that which it sometimes seems we're due to lose. Uncompromising perhaps, he was one of a series of writers dismayed by modernity at large, not least the unthinking ugliness that so often mars what apparent necessity can claim. What verdict would he lay now upon the new estates, so boxy and so regular, springing up throughout the woods and Weald of Sussex and Surrey? It is not hard to imagine. More heartening, and hopefully more enduring, are his thoughts on the Downs themselves, both north and south of the Weald. Belloc asked why it was that, though they were not high, they achieved majesty. 'Something of that economy and reserve by whose power the classic in verse or architecture grows upon the mind is present in the Downs. These which we had travelled that day were not my own hills… but they were similar because they stood up above the sand and the pines, and because they were of that white barren soil, clothed in close turf, wherein nothing but the beech, the yew, and our own affection can take root and grow.'

I got to the vista at Ranmore Common to see a child playing with a kite with their mother while a pensioner painted, rooted enough to almost be part of the landscape and there it was – the view over the Weald, cinematically tinted in the early evening light. It was a view to take in in great lungfuls, the boundless trees, the distant blue of the Belloc's own Downs, the golden green air all urging to stop and keep going at once.

A couple of mountain bikers in skater-type black helmets were drinking tea from paper cups with plastic lids. My worries over water, which had plagued me over the course of the afternoon, were now at an end. Here, at the café-soon-to-be-revealed, I could drink tea after tea, possibly down a flapjack and replenish at last my rapidly-emptying water bottles. All I had to do was walk a little further and, so confident was I of my sudden success, I didn't stop to ask the bikers where the café was. It was probably bespoke and aluminium, a trailer deposited and hitched at the beginning and end of each lengthy summer's day, some sage or starry-eyed attendee who would pass me my quota of caffeine with a look of wisdom and respect.

But it wasn't there. Further along the track that wended its way across the buoyant green turf of the common, over the little road, there was just no café to be found. And the mountain bikers were quarter of a mile behind me now – too far, it felt, to retrace my steps. The church I'd seen on the map, at the beginning of the common's open pasture, had yielded no tap, only a bench occupied by a couple of sarcastic teenagers and a large plastic green barrel whose water was murky and stank. There was nothing for it but to push on to Box Hill.

A tarmaced road devoid of traffic led me down besides a landrover pulling the kind of passenger train I'd last seen on Eastbourne beachfront, now utterly vacated of punters as it struggled up the hill. The driver looked at me slightly accusatory or perhaps just embarrassed. There must have been some kind of race here recently as someone had daubed on the road; 'DOG' in large white letters and, later; 'GO HARRY!'.

To my right stretched one of the biggest vineyards in Southern England, lending feelings of exoticism and mild displacement. I experienced curious visual effects as the lines of vines rolled by in highly mathematical perspective. 'The Old Road in crossing a valley always chooses a place where some spur of high land leads down to the river...' wrote Belloc, his words echoing in my ears like some kind of Edwardian Ben Kenobi, '...and corresponds to a dry rise immediately upon the other bank... '. There would be a rise alright. Box Hill loomed ahead.

Over an A road, past a carpark with an ice cream van quite useless now, I found myself at the edge of the Mole river, stepping stones dotted across, just as in the picture on the cover of my little pilgrims' guide. It was an iconic symbol of the route and I was glad now that I'd come this way, that I hadn't succumbed - or been in a position to succumb to – Dorking's apparently elegant charms.

The Mole may take its name from its rumoured ability to disappear underground, or at least to have underground sections capable of swallowing whole trees. It was something to think about as I made my way across the concrete stones, a little slippery and my pack as heavy and ungainly as ever though the water looked shallow enough. It was a pretty scene that let you think you were in some kind of photo yourself, the image captured in the memory's eye, the overhanging trees all subdued hues, the water brown with the shade and the gravelly bed. There was a feeling of reflection amid stepping towards completion of a semi-mythologised goal. And then the climb.

It was probably the steepest ascent on the route, such as it was, some 260 or so steps and I was met at every turn by comments and looks of alarm or sympathy if not actual muted derision upon the size of my pack. When I finally did reach the top, probably somewhat purple-faced as I sat on a bench, a lithe, conventional couple in sneakers and their twenties bounced past; the woman, with closely cropped brown hair proclaiming "easy!" in my direction, just about successfully suppressing a sneer.

Then the crowd and the view, a balloon going up on the horizon. Everything had taken on a slightly surreal quality. I seemed to be surrounded by the French. It was one of those views where you don't know what to take in first until you are absorbed into the vista of trees upon trees, a kind of near seascape as if the light of the leaves is reflected. I left with a feeling of expansion, my mind belittled by the miles to the south and suddenly pleasantly irrelevant.

Aware of the looming last light, I pushed on to the pub. I walked along a busy metalled road through more woods for several hundred metres, beginning to despair of my finding the place at all. But then there it was, 'The Smith and Western Bar Grill Diner.' The carpark was full of Humvee-like Chelsea tractors and the place itself was styled like an old ranch – a veranda with tables with green and white cloths, hurricane lamps on the walls and, inside, bar staff with full cowboy and cowgirl costumes. I wasn't in

Hampshire anymore.

The menu board had lots of spare rib options, very pricey. I thought sitting outside might be pleasant enough as internally the place was heaving with families, fully decibelled. It was drinks only outside so I dutifully bought a lime soda, which made the barmaid pull a face, as well as the pint, and had my bottles filled. I couldn't bear the thought of eating there with so much noise and little headspace and swiftly downed my drink outside in the gathering dusk.

A nearby footpath led me north into the woods. I branched off from the path till I found some scraggy little yews next to the remains of a stick bivouac, having nearly set up near a tractor and woodpile. It was a reminder that, when seeking sanctuary away from a path you have to make sure you don't camp nearer to another path in the process. A few walkers came by, near, but not near enough to see me. I had time to set up, eat my ration of instant pasta and tuna on my little meths burner and get a fire together before it got properly dark.

It was an hour or two later as I sat with my thoughts, that I thought I heard a man's voice, calling out seemingly close. I didn't think much of it but couldn't help a few scenarios bounce round my brain. Should I have texted my whereabouts to a friend a little earlier? Had I somehow made myself conspicuous? That late in the season it was still a long night in the tent and I felt too bloody minded to put the fire out, as part of me wanted to do, to be on the safe side.

Presently, the sound of crashing in the undergrowth and the faint, purple light of a not-very-powerful torch announced somebody coming down the footpath. I hastily tried to break up the fire but as the flames on the branches I waved refused to go out I realised it was too late for such attempts at the clandestine. The blue, purple light from the footpath came towards me. Was my number finally up?

Was I about to be dispatched, some hiking horror story statistic? At best, I thought the encounter was due to be stressful. I braced myself, reached for my staff to find it was still by the tent – some yards and precious seconds away.

A big guy stumbled into the firelight, in a tracksuit. It turned out he was Asian, bemused by my attempts to hide the fire and not unfriendly. A taxi driver, it turned out he loved Box Hill and had come here today for perspective, to see if the hill could help tell him what had been going on these last few days; could help him find some meaning of his sense of something in the air.

He'd sat by a tree, just out of the firelight so that I could no longer see him, only hear his seemingly disembodied voice. He'd got drunk and stoned and fallen asleep, which accounted for his now nocturnal wander in the woods. He feigned drowsiness, yawning, but I could hear him twanging the ringpull on his last remaining can of beer in agitation and I was yet to properly establish whether or not he could be a threat. But he was harmless. I offered him bread and cheese when he talked about my cooking 'a tasty dish' but he politely refused, said he had some stuff back in his car.

Scenarios bouldered through my mind. I didn't particularly want him hanging around by my camp as I didn't think I could relax with the knowledge of him there. His repeatedly pinging the ringpull made me unsure as to whether or not he might be a bit deranged. But equally, my having left the original footpath and not knowing where the nearer one went meant my trying to find his car with him would probably only result in the pair of us getting lost, memories of a night in the woods above Sidmouth where my torch died in the rain and it took me several soggy hours to find my tent not far from my mind. In the event, as I deliberated, the taxi-driver got up and wandered off into the woods, leaving me feeling I'd done him a proper disservice. I stayed up for a good while after his departure but he didn't return. The sound of owls, a large dog fox and possibly a stag punctuated the rest of the night. I had some way to go to make amends.

Two Swords

Henry II was never a man who liked to relinquish control. This was particularly apparent when it came to law and order. He saw himself as the living embodiment of a return to the stability of his grandfather Henry I's day after the intervening strife of Stephen and Matilda's civil war. His court was the very centre of a Twelfth Century renaissance; a whole host of writers flourished in his rule, scholars flocked to the country, the production of books and illuminated manuscripts cranked up significantly, architecture was influenced by contact with the Moors, hospitals, leper colonies, churches, abbeys, bridges, kitchens, palaces and hunting lodges all sprang up during the years of his reign. Some £20,000 was spent on the repair or construction of castles at the same time.

But Henry's legal reforms and aspirations perhaps defined the early years of his rule. He saw his obligations as those of any prince to rule justly. By working with and improving English law and an English system of justice he could associate himself with the fabled Anglo-Saxon kings. Trial by jury was made available for civil cases relating to property and he sought to improve the efficiency of the judicial system by rooting out corruption. It is said he did more to promote the rule of law in England than any other monarch before or since. But one issue rankled for Henry more than most. During the civil war, much power had ceded to Rome and the Church and Henry was determined to regain it. Nowhere was this more starkly illustrated than over the issue of criminous clerks.

At this time clergy were not subject to trial and punishment by secular courts, being dealt with in Church courts characterised for some by their leniency. Many students, accountants, clerks and doctors part of 'minor orders' of the clergy came under this system. In Norman times, violent crime among clergy had been treated in secular courts - this formed another part of Henry's narrative that he was trying to restore a sense of former order. Ultimately, he wanted a central legal system under his control; to do away with Church courts altogether, or at least to amalgamate the two.

For Becket, it was an equally existential issue but for entirely different reasons. His metamorphosis after his consecration as archbishop can be seen as chiefly intellectual rather than, or as well as, spiritual. He was heavily influenced by Salisbury, who drew upon Robert of Melun's theories of resistance to a tyrant. The two agreed that infringements on the Church's liberties were an insult to God. 'A good pastor,' Melun had written, 'should resist a wicked ruler who stubbornly refuses to mend his ways even to the point of martyrdom.'

Becket would soon proclaim to the pope that 'what is Caesar's must be rendered unto Caesar', but that which was appropriated by a secular ruler above his legal due 'belongs not to Caesar but a tyrant'. For Becket it had become like John the Baptist and that other great autocrat King Herod all over again. For just as John the Baptist had confronted Herod, if Henry harassed the Church, Becket would have no choice but to take him to task. It has been said this resolution marked the true change in Becket after he took the archbishopric, over and above his religious transformation. But did he reflect even then how it had ended for St John?

The clouds gathered pace when Becket preached before Henry in London in July 1163. He took as his text '"Look, Lord, here are two swords." And he said to them, "It is enough"'; a classic allegory for the powers of popes and kings, implying the former effectively held the higher authority. In the Biblical story the disciples had shown Jesus two swords after the Last Supper. 'It is enough', he had said, later ordering St. Peter to sheathe one of them.

It was as clear a sign of the shift in Becket's sensibilities as anything previously and Henry appeared not to take it in good humour. When a judgement subsequently went in the king's favour over a priest returned for trial, who was charged with murdering a knight, Henry pressed his advantage, demanding the death penalty and an oath from the bishops that they did not spare the man because of his station. Becket protested and responded by excommunicating one of Henry's men. The king rode to Windsor in disgust, stating 'Now I have no more love of him.' It was a precursor to the coming storm.

+   +   +

I woke up to the sound of workmen whistling by the tractor, still – it turned out – not far away from my camp. I packed up quietly and left surreptitiously in the opposite direction, finding my way back to the road by obscure paths, mist dripping from the trees. As my little toe was now quite bad; a little gammy, soft where the skin had lifted off and in danger of splitting, I was planning to head for Reigate and get a train home but a friend via text urged me on and I knew she was right. I'd spend a night or two in the town, rest up a little in a B & B or some such establishment, though quite how I'd afford it was anyone's guess.

I dutifully left the North Downs Way some miles further, after looking back though a gap in the trees to a receding Box Hill, the line of hills to the south west just visible, their tops just clear of the otherwise enveloping mist, like little islands. I came to a little B-road till the path led down a beech-lined shaw, processional, after which I took my leave. The path took me to Buckland village where, appropriately, the Post Office-come-deli-come-antiques emporium supplied me with another necessary second breakfast. Then the path led by a large pond and through a golf course until I reached the minor roadway of a holloway; proper and rooted and deep, sloping down towards Reigate in a kind of natural stateliness.

My little book said Henry had stopped in the town on his pilgrimage after Becket's martyrdom. Specifically, a tradition has it he stayed at the Red Cross Inn, so I determined to try and find the place, sans smart phone, not really fancying my chances. But perhaps I'd be able to spend the night there if I was successful. It seemed as good an idea as any. The town marks the halfway point between Winchester and Canterbury and may have been named for its royal connection ('king-street' could be a possible interpretation of its name, though 'where the roe-deer sported' is a more popular take). Still, the name did not appear until a few years after Becket's murder, leading some to associate the place specifically with Henry's journey. Belloc was convinced the place would have formed a general resting place, as evidenced by St Thomas's chapel, which stood where the town hall can now be found.

Whether or not he stayed in the town, Henry's route to Canterbury was convoluted and, to modern would-be observers, obscure. He was meant to have landed at Southampton in July 1174 and rode eastwards, having spent a suitable time lying low in Ireland where he used the time for some casual subjugation before more fighting on the Continent. The little evidence of his pilgrimage route that survives implies he might have spent the night in London – expenses for the hire of horses for sailors to follow him there have been recorded. Henry was meant to have travelled at speed, largely avoiding towns and it has been said that an

101

eager medieval traveller on horseback could cover 30-40 miles a day, which would fit with the five days of travel it took Henry to reach Canterbury. It is feasible at least that he might have used the Pilgrims' Way, though Dean Stanley, who is credited as inspiring both Belloc and Captain James, suggested he used a road that traversed the Surrey Hills and dropped into Canterbury by Harbledown on the London Road where reliable documentation catches up with the King. An alternative to the Roman roads would apparently have been preferable for anyone on horseback.

Reading though the minutia of the historiography of the route of pilgrims in general and that of the Pilgrims' Way in particular, it's easy to feel we begin to miss the point. A detour to Reigate didn't feel so very off route to me, it certainly wasn't to Belloc, and it seems likely enough that many pilgrims would make use of towns along the way, though some, peasants seeking to avoid restrictions on movement perhaps, may have tried to keep their heads down. There's a valid case for tracing the route, but to pin the existence of pilgrims upon any given route's veracity can give grounds for exasperation with overly pedantic antiquarians.

The Red Cross had changed its name apparently, though still retained the symbol of its sign so that tracking it down would be doubly hard. A surprise then when the very first building I faced at the edge of town after the holloway was the very same Red Cross, repatriated to its original name, unlikely in black and white cladding, a little dilapidated and visibly promising Sky Sports but there all the same at the foot of my path. There was nobody there but the barmaid, who took my request for a lime soda with by-now-unusual good grace. Old, flagged flooring and suitably ancient-looking tables added to a sense of ambience along with the remains of a very old door now pinned to one wall. There was a very real feel that a king might have stayed here, like he could at any moment stride through the weathered wood of the trophy-like entrance.

Redhill – down the road from Reigate - was a little cheaper for accommodation according to the barmaid. I dutifully headed east. I stocked up on food in a supermarket, adjusting to the town rules where nobody says hello, acquiring a somewhat large bag. Pasta packs and sachets of tuna greeted my eye in the supermarket without too much effort but by the time I emerged and had scored a tea in the café underneath what had once been the market hall I felt stressed. I hadn't really thought matters through. I didn't have the cash to stay anywhere even if I found somewhere cheap. I hadn't withdrawn the last of my money in my paypal account and the supermarket had made a huge dint in financial resources. The bank couldn't help and the library, when I found it, was shut.

Not really knowing what to do next I carried on walking. At a junction on a busy road I realised I could take a less-used road to a good bit of woodland the other side of Redhill. I got a tea in a large pub where I somehow managed to convince a hesitant Australian - who'd been turning the air less than respectable with his stories of conquests of women – to let me use his phone to transfer the last of my money. He and his drinking companion wished me luck, with a good-natured sincerity I found disarming, and I left with far greater peace of mind.

A cashpoint down the way confirmed my success and soon I was heading out down 'Philanthropic Road' and other minor lanes till I got to a farm shop on the site of an old priory, now a hotel - a likely sign of vindication of Belloc's theory of the stopover here - and I talked for a while with a black-haired girl at the cheese counter with the most startling blue eyes. The wood was only up the road, behind a little band of houses on an A-road. Skirting along a raised track I dropped down into a beautiful grove of birches, feeling relatively secluded and somewhat saved. Here was a place I could rest. Confetti of the yellow leaves, falling in the wind and steady sun put me at ease. Rooks tumbled through with the twilight, roosting above me, fraternal.

At some stage that evening, as I sat by the fire, something large made footfall behind me. I turned but could see nothing, just felt a presence, could almost feel the animal's breath; pregnant, expectant, half-startled like me. It seemed to speak of everything that had happened during this stage of the walk – the knowledge of the new Western intervention against Isis, my thoughts on St Martha's, my resolution to try and move on. And with it the hope of the walk, the sense of things being lifted up, the sense of still-unproven potential. Before me now was the animal kingdom; hidden but heavy with questions. Whatever it was, it was large and very possibly a deer. As I reached for my staff, I heard it turn and bolt off, every bit as close as I had reckoned.

I rested up the following day, my back to a birch, writing up notes. My toe had begun to split a little so I kept it clean and dry and used some iodine spray. The night before, I'd dreamed of a wolfhound with a burning paw. Later, I hobbled to a nearby pub, putting weight on my bad foot only with difficulty, despite a fresh blister pack. After stopping the previous night, my toe had smelt high when I took off the dressing. The remaining sixty miles seemed suddenly further than ever.

After a meal in the pub, I found a café called 'Heaven' which was part of some healing clinic, tables in a little courtyard with plants growing up the slate walls with a water feature in a tiered arrangement, a feeling of proper arrival. It was almost hallucinatory. 'Limpsfield', nearby, pointed to the possibility of pilgrims in the past, similarly footsore. I dreamed that, after an amazing sunset, Harry Potter was drinking a little whiskey with his friends from out the back of a van in a park though whether in celebration or to steady his nerves was not exactly clear.

I woke before dawn and ran through lyrics in my head as I lay with the flap to my tent open to take in the first of the light, bathed in the noise of the rooks. It was threatening rain so I tatted down early and got onto the road – literally the A-road by the houses. I'd been able to hear the M23 and M25 from my camp, their junction a mile or so off, but most of the noise was from the nearer thoroughfare. Still, it was a sign I'd made it halfway – I was due north of Brighton. I thought about going home. My clothes were crawling, the state of my toe seemed unnegotiable despite my having bandaged it and I didn't object with myself. It would be easy now to take a bus into Redhill and hop on a train. But then again, if my toe held out till the nearby train station, perhaps I could continue.

I walked up to Blacklands Meadow – shrubby, returning to woodland. The rain duly kicked in and, in order to continue, I had to crawl under half-fallen aspens. The path ran out into walls of brambles twice amid the low wood before I returned to the original path which I'd abandoned as it had been going south. But it turned around and led me over open fields as the rain eased off.

After crossing a road, the sun came out and I spent a mile singing, decided to carry on past the path to the station, my heart lifting with the prospect of being able to carry on. I wanted to do so for all of my friends, I knew it was the best thing I could possibly do and to suddenly have the prospect of finishing the walk this year could only make me feel euphoric. The road took me over the motorway junction, strange and jarring of course, and I carried on down a lane at the base of the ridge to avoid the climb; cars, vans and trucks annoying but not an immediate threat to my life. But when I got to end of the lane and was back on a track without much traffic, my toe gave out, like it had split afresh, ruptured, and

I was reduced to an instant slow limp. I made my way, slow and painful, down to a suburban station a couple of miles into the outskirts of Croydon, along past the lines of the stock-broker houses, a teenager in a car with fluffy dice sneering at me.

Nonetheless, the next day, at home, I sat on a bench in the park, still only able to walk very slowly, feeling more peaceful than at any time I could immediately remember. My home town, the market town, propitious on a hill and by a river felt unusually welcoming. It was the end of the season now, there'd be no big walks for the rest of year. I could only tell myself I'd done my best, trying to sweeten the pill. Still, a happy-sounding raven sang from a tree. The sun shone on the trees by the river, the sound of a balalaika drifted up the water from the high street. I hobbled around. It was good to be back. But this obviously wasn't the end. In a dream, where activist friends were cooks, somebody mixed a restorative brew. It was chiefly for my benefit, to get me back to where I ought to be. I tried fixing my sights on horizons, though Spring was a long way away.

The Borders

I came back the Pilgrims' Way the following summer. It was a time of truly new beginnings. I seemed to have weathered the worst of the winter storms, both those of the literal weather and other more personal squalls.

But I was spurred by the need to escape – to escape what felt a practical incarceration in a flat that, however practical, however propitious, had such a literally 'flat' feel, a large part of me still despised. Or perhaps I still despised myself for living there. I'd come home from gigs, rendezvous, long walks elated only to feel my sense of joy or inspiration stutter out upon the shoals of a concrete-encased feeling of sterility. I'd open the windows both front and back with the beginning of Spring, launch day-long blitzes on accumulating detritus, fumigate the place with incense and sage but I was simply shoring the sides. Trying to keep my head psychologically above water, I felt I was swimming upstream. Bleak dreams haunted my nights.

There were other needs for escape. I was caught in a dilemma; still on the mentally-scouring heavy sleeping pills, I was told that I ought to avoid stress. But the campaigning against fracking was in full flight. I was being asked up to training weekends in London, people very publicly added me to burgeoning groups, the government seemed set on fracking whatever the cost or outcry and it was truly a maddening prospect. It came down to a very simple choice; to continue campaigning, even if only through writing or keep my head down and try to produce another book. Somehow though the environmentalism had its own seemingly inescapable logic or sense of stark necessity. And now the government was poised to poison the water.

Looking away felt unthinkable and yet I had already clearly run myself into the ground. I'd poured my all into the campaign. But was I really serving the earth by locking myself away infront of a computer, casting out my energy like a wave at high tide over the shoals of obligation, every effort seemingly only fuelling further demands? I continued with the writing course but I was caught between two streams; expectation and a need for greater harmony. Something, it seemed, had to give.

Feeling increasingly frayed, I had spent a weekend out in a village at the foot of the Downs that I knew, staying in a friend's shepherd's hut. It was very early Spring. Rooks gathered high in the still-bare branches of nearby, towering ash trees. Tribes of finches and tits mobbed a nearby elder bush on a regular basis. I cooked on the kippering heat of the tiny, efficient stove and read Satish Kumar and some of my host's mini library.

The first night there I had a feeling of deep peace, like I was being held by something infinitely greater than me, a sense of total immanence. I slept better than I had for days. Just to have been able to hear the wider world by night was a paradigm shift from the closed, silent air of my flat. My life back there felt more than ever a half-life, all my instincts about the place confirmed. But with the property market seemingly sewn up, other options were thin on the ground. The prospect of a life in sheds seemed suddenly more amenable. "Less is more" as someone had written in the hut's visitor's book.

And reading one of my host's books, another thing became clear; that nature writing was a form of praise. Looking for spiritual practise, I was torn between a politics which once had seemed so benevolent and righteous and the urge for creativity. I wanted to engage in something other than rhetorical exploits, to rise above a burden of responsibility I hadn't fully realised I was lining myself up for. Perhaps this; to write of the things that I loved, was the best thing I could possibly do.

Such sensibilities had been a huge inspiration for leaving the southern city, a few years after my sojourns up North, after the madness of the invasion of Iraq, after my near-total breakdown. Friends had moved further out to the village here when I'd moved to the intervening market town. I'd trekked out here every week to rehearse, over the fields from the nearest train station, the old quarrymen's village there archaically beautiful, framed by little rolling slopes of pasture as the Downs themselves, always familiar, stood sentinel on my other side, like I, prodigal, had finally come home. I sat beneath oaks in parkland with tomes on the landscape, preparing to study, not then aware that one day soon I'd have to choose my path with greater clarity. It was only now, years later, that the full consequences of that choice were coming home.

As I left the village after the stay in the hut, I met a carpenter friend and ex-bandmate who I suddenly saw, or understood, more clearly than ever; a product perhaps of my liminal state and the effect of being semi-outdoors for several days. We used to rehearse in her Eighteenth Century workshop, all aging brick and voluminous white windows. Sawdust everywhere in the workshop itself, we crammed in the little adjoining estate museum, full of photos, maps and antiquated tools. Seeing her that morning as I walked through the village for the bus, I could see the extent to which she was a part of this very ancient world, through habit and allegiance, counterpoised against the kind of reality that I was now trying to outrun. And perhaps, to see me like this, newly nomadic, a pack on my back again, she saw a little more of who I once was, of who I was still meant to be.

My mental state still fraught, a friend paid for me to go on a residential walking week in Devon. It couldn't have been better timed or more necessary. I felt on the brink of going downhill. It could be a long way down, as I knew, and the week – in a beautiful old Georgian House near Dartmoor, with twice-daily meditation sessions and guided walks every day, every detail taken care of - made me feel on the cusp of having been institutionalised. But I wasn't of course; the week was a saviour, the company sound and the walking incredible. On our final day we walked across a moor in the sun to a gigantic tor, castle-like, stood with the view and this I knew, again, was how redemption felt. I felt highly blessed and as aware as ever of those in society who had not been given such Godsends and spiralled into incarceration when all they really needed was a little structure and genuine sanctuary. In all my years since being in hospital, it was the closest I'd come to re-admission.

Driven, having had to stop the writing course because of my health and with the prospect of deferment uncertain, I sought out pastures new. I headed to a friend's in a town in Somerset, self-consciously 'hip' but still genuinely beguiling. A little stream ran down the middle of one of the main streets, boutique shops lined others. The monthly market was spectacular. And the feel of being in the West again was visceral, like a summer sunrise I thought I had forgotten, a sense of being part of the world once again, a sense of being back in the folds of humanity and the living land.

Exploring still, I headed up into the Welsh Borders to visit the last place I'd lived before I'd returned to life in houses. I took a train to a town where I used to go busking, full of ancient timber-framed buildings and replete with medieval castle and walked west, along a path that would take two or three days to reach my former home. I'd lived in the woods there with friends from Newbury, in the summer and autumn after the campaign, living on the edge of oak coppice on a small, steep hill, looking out back over

England while in the other direction mountains rolled away in unlikely peaks, lit pink and orange with watery sunsets. But I'd become unwell there, after my frugal summer walking and busking and minimal food. The full impact of events were catching up with me and copious hash and a little pinch of mushrooms did little to help, neither did attempting to still live off busking and living with people who, in unlikely and unnecessary bonfires, burnt all the wood I was gathering for a winter everyone said would be harsh. The busking town was thirty miles away, a difficult and increasingly chaotic weekly hitch. Too proud to sign on, I wasn't sure exactly how I'd make it through the coming months. And the trauma of losing the landscapes I had known sat with me, bewildering. I'd sit by the river and weep, without really knowing why.

But I'd felt at home there, was more than glad to live on the land, sharing a bender, walking the hills; bigger than those I was accustomed to, rough and exhilarating, actual highlands behind us in a broad bow we would walk to other woodland over; the valley stretching out below, impossibly verdant, golden and green with the rain, hues of blue and patched like an intricate cloth. It felt like this could just be the beginning, a foundation that would not be removed. As the trees turned to burgeoning gold, vivid in the air all around me, myself almost a part of their movement, their life, I didn't think it was possible to feel so alive.

On one of my last days there, I sat on a stile as two men in tweeds made their way over a meadow towards me, one of them with a hawk on his arm. I looked in its eyes as they passed and it stared back at me, splayed its wings only inches away from my face. Golden globes shone back at me, like the colour and vibrancy of the leaves on the hill, my own eyes now full of a similar life and just for a moment I didn't know if I was looking at the hawk or if he was me returning my gaze. A horse-drawn couple came to the hill with two

111

horses, one black, one white on the lively green mounds of the hillside, framing my walks like something from a story of the Grail.

We'd been beginning to build a treehouse hotel; the place would be used as a kind of retreat. The very first house would be my new home; a platform strung between the rectangle of four young oaks, after weeks of steady work finally had a tarp placed over the barreltop-like hazel of the roof. In one end we'd placed three long, reclaimed windows with white wooden frames. In the other a little African-like doorway led to a short sitting-ledge. I envisioned a kind of circular filing cabinet hung from the hazel where I could store any information to be accessed at will. Middle-class, middle aged hikers found me wide-eyed in the greenery, asked if I was Dr Livingstone.

But waking one morning, an early Autumn storm was getting up. I rose as if elemental myself and climbed up to see the corners of the platform pounding against the lagging between them and the still-living bark. The treehouse was suspended from the four oaks in a rough quadrangle. In order to reduce the strain on the supporting trees, each corner of the treehouse had been hung from stout rope, to give the trees a little more movement. Now the carpet lagging lashed in to protect the trees where they met the structure was being worn thin as I watched. I took down the roof there and then and we winched down the platform soon after. It felt like my dreams were dissolving. But in a sense, after Newbury, I often carried with me a sense that whatever I'd try to establish - be it a home or lasting relationship - would only ever be taken away. I'd move, cut my ties before I got stung.

The constant sound of chainsaws in the woods, still redolent of carnage and evictions at that point, and our being used as target practise by the RAF - harriers routinely pouring over the tops of the trees - helped finished the work. Liminal, not sleeping, my mind at times was like a radio receiver, tuning in to conversations from Irish voices; cathartic, placatory. The storm raged. Everything felt turbulent. We sheltered under my tarp, but the wind was still harrying, like being at sea. I thought it was the end of Time. The RAF pressed home their advantage, two planes at once striking over the hill not shy of air brakes. My landlady cooked me a meal in the shed, the first proper meal that I'd eaten for what seemed like weeks and I talked of harriers, other birds of prey and Merlin himself and it felt like I was dropping revelations. The RAF planes were subsequently replaced by droning gliders, not sinister then, a sudden softness in the soundscape of the sky like the world was suddenly trying to ameliorate my distress.

When my parents came for me, my father parked his white BMW in the meadow at the bottom of the hill, sat in it with the doors open like it was a steed or chariot. I straddled a barred gate on my belly, agonised, knowing on some level exactly what was going on. I knew how precious this place was to me. I knew if I went that I might never see it again, that I might never be the same person. They told me we were going to buy vegetables. I only got out three hundred miles later. Hospitalisation and a return to life in houses ensued. In some respects, the wound had never healed.

I sat at the top of the hill upon re-arrival at that place, back to a fence post, exhausted, presently made my way along the track to an old wooden shed where we'd once got water. It was pristine then, a new build, weather-boarded and golden, roof replete with freshly-minted shingles. It looked a little dilapidated now, plywood patching the floor but still the sense of homecoming was profound. I stayed for two or three weeks. My old landlady was breeding Hebridean sheep and their brown, horned forms dotted the hillside, staring up at me over the fences, yellow-eyed and strangely enthusiastic as I practised my pipes, looking back over the once-so-familiar view. We drank and played music and somehow I didn't need to take the sleeping pills.

But there was nowhere really established to move to, my talk of staying any longer was never discussed and I didn't want to outstay my welcome. Besides, the writing course felt like unfinished business and I only had a limited window of time with return train tickets. When the crew there joked that they'd thought I was special forces when I'd rocked up with my one-man tent, in a way that implied that they might have been actually serious, I thought it was time to head home.

That spring the Tories were returned to power in the general election. More than a Conservative victory, it was a decimation of the English Left. Bands of rain swept the high street as I sat beneath the awning of a café, disconsolate. But after a friend's gig a searchlight scoured the city sky like somebody was looking for some sign of hope. A woman on the bridge sang 'Amazing Grace'. I was accepted back on the writing course.

I was on the brink of returning to the Pilgrims' Way but once again the sleepers interfered. As before, I headed to the Forest. As I set out from the spa town, I exchanged perfunctory greetings with a labourer whose collie was busy biting the shovelfuls of flying dirt he was shifting. I camped in a wood choked with rhododendron, just about finding a little scrap of untouched outgrown chestnut coppice to pitch up in after some effort.

I had a book of Sussex tales on me, including a passage from my old English teacher-come-professional-storyteller who said you often get lost in the Forest – there was a byelaw preventing the footpaths being overly marked – but you just had to follow your nose. Which was just as well as the

114

following day I lost my way almost immediately. Decidedly off-piste, herds of fallow deer announced themselves, including one creature who peered at me over the ferns, ears pointed eagerly for all the world like some kind of native kangaroo. Others grazed beneath oaks, melted away into the treeline when they literally got wind of me. Later, a casual half dozen, sleek and light, their backs all auburn and brown, their sides and underbellies the colour of cream bounded off uphill in such a tight mass it was impossible to count them, their heads just visible momentarily above the line of the crest of the hill, floating like fairground attractions. Just after, a fox ran out, low legged with a massive brush, relaxed and single minded. Life was suddenly good.

I found my way to a grove of beeches marked on my friend's map, got there relatively early and sang and learnt songs for hours, nobody there but a few roaming deer close by, half oblivious, a few walkers out and about from the village down the hill. There was a tangible sense of arrival, of being more fully alive, rendered all the more intense for being on my own with nothing to do except sing and wander among the towering beech groves, the most beautiful I'd ever seen, huge maiden trees stood separate, separated by smaller trees and bushes so that they kept court in little interlocking pockets of wide space. I left after dawn, walked down the hill by a golf course shrouded in the early-morning mist. "Tom White on a bike?" asked a lad of his friend on an industrial estate in the ensuing village, in something of a state of amazement. "On a mountain bike? Tom White was riding a bike!" I didn't know it then but I had finally come home. It seemed a time of minor miracles.

Back to Merstham

I walked out of my front door and down to the high street, where I picked up a small loaf of bread and said a prayer for my journey in a little chapel, boarding a train not long after. At the connection at Redhill I looked out from the still-open door of my just-boarded train to see a poem on the wall of the platform directly opposite me. It was called 'Dragons' and by an eleven-year-old girl. There was something about a Bat King. The train pulled away as I was halfway though it. It said we would just about make it.

At Merstham, after I alighted, an old guy with a thin and leathery-looking face outside a greasy spoon looked at me jaundiced and bitter. I put my head down and kept going. The motorway felt like more of an afront than I remembered it. Then I was retracing my steps up a gentle hill full of burgeoning wheat, sat for a while at the top near a whitewashed trigpoint by a broad and strangely oak-like ash. Far away, just visible, stood the towers of the City of London, literally citadel-like from such a distance and seeming strangely peaceful. Those towers of glass were frenetic of course as was the rest of the place but here no sound of that could come to me.

It was as remote as another world, just as it had been most of my life. A traveller girl I'd met before I'd gone on the road had said you could lose yourself in London, echoing the lyrics of an ambient track of the day and I'd stayed away for years. I wondered briefly how many old school friends now worked in those grinding mills of commerce but found it was easier simply to stare at the sky, to think about walking, make the most of my time out in the air. If riches could ever be measured, I felt fabulously wealthy under that ash.

The ensuing lane had a few grand, probably stock-brokers' houses, testaments to capital, red bricked and palatial, or pseudo-Tudor, behind iron gates, tidy-lawned with immaculate hedges. Just as a succession of white vans hectoring past was beginning to get on my nerves, the path headed off the road down through overshadowing yews and dense hazel, intermingled with a few beeches and wild service trees. For most of the rest of the day I walked through woods with the M25 a constant companion, only a field or two away down to my right.

Before the turning, on a lane, I passed a man in an England sweater, jogging with a ginger dog. Another indifferent dog with a half-friendly, half-bemused owner. By a meadow to the south a couple were lying out flat besides one another, kissing, engrossed. A girl came along being pulled by an English sheep dog, two friends behind her laughing, for reasons unknown. A little freestanding tap, seemingly placed there primarily for the benefit of dogs, sated my need for fresh water.

More woods, the path dropping down to cross a dual carriageway, a warehouse and yard for Britannia Lorries, an office in a little grotto in the woods, incongruous, round and glass and modern; a couple of men, spindly in suits, at their desks. It lay in one of the chalk pits that lie upon or nearby the route for much of the way here. Chalk was quarried widely from the 1840's and burnt to make lime for decorating, mortar and as a fertilizer. Chalk, Belloc states, 'should be warmly hymned and praised by every man who belongs to south England, for it is the meaning of the good land... Every one brought up among the chalk pits remembers them more vividly than any other thing about his home, and when he returns from some exile he catches the feeling of his boyhood as he sees them far off upon the hills.'

In this respect at least I was a true southerner. I knew

the hillforts Belloc sang the praise of, and which were founded on the chalk, knew how 'its lonely breadths delight us when the white clouds and the flocks move over them together'. At the top of the hill I grew up on, a string of minor chalk pits, now largely grown over into Tolkienesque hills and hollows formed a backdrop to my younger years. But too, I thought of those inhabitants who'd known the forts and tracks as keenly, drove their cattle, quite possibly charioteered upon the sheep-cropped plains, the thought of their presence almost familiar, a thing that I could understand, perhaps because I pined for other countries, other peoples, perhaps because the green of the hills called like some other half-forgotten promise, perhaps because I knew I'd have to leave in order to belong.

I stopped about half three in some woods that seemed peaceful and inviting, feeling slightly stressed. Hopping a fence, I sat beneath beeches and conifers until it felt slightly oppressive so I pitched up a bit further on, with more light and a thick mast of beech leaves though as it turned out I was right next to the path, albeit less frequented now. The roar of the M25 was incessant, lapsing in and out of my consciousness. I was a little concerned the road would be equally apparent the whole of the rest of the way but there was nothing I could do about that now. The sound seemed to reach out and mar the surrounding landscape as it snaked its way past, across a field flushed green with young wheat, the road ubiquitous here for better or worse. I had no real appetite which wasn't a good sign. But I was glad to stop for the day and the spot felt homely despite the motorway, there in the beeches on a knoll like I was some kind of sentry at my post. I tried not to think of the election, called friends I'd been meaning to speak to for ages. Despite being tired I had a feeling of momentum and satisfaction.

From here to much further east the motorway, whether the M25, M26 or M20, follows the line of the North Downs to a surprising degree, albeit south of the hilltops, down in the vale. It's a sign perhaps of the route's still current validity, following as it does the crossing place of the Channel to the heart of country inland. Early prehistoric man making his way before and after the last ice age does not at first glance have much in common with the thousands hemmed in in little blatting boxes but our general trends still endure; the urge or need to travel and migrate. Only the speed and means have changed. But for all the apparent convenience, can we really say we're better off, more civilised, more free?

There are older dichotomies. Cobbett was never a fan of the turnpikes that had grown up all over the country, from the Seventeenth Century but reaching their peak during Cobbett's own day in the early Eighteen Hundreds. These new roads were tolled at special gates as a means of supporting their newly invigorated upkeep. Prior to this, maintenance had been the responsibility of parish and private enterprise and – not least – the monasteries. After the dissolution the results were patchy at best. The turnpikes were perhaps the most systematic overhaul of the English road network since the Romans. While they practically revolutionised road travel for many, toll-keepers could be petty and many saw their fines and delays as an affront to liberty itself. At times the gates were smashed and toll-keepers attacked by rioters disguised as women; the disturbances consequently known as "Rebecca Riots".

The roads were still a relative innovation in Cobbett's day and were being constantly added to. He would often make diversions of several miles in order to avoid the gates where the levies were charged. In their heyday some 24,599 miles of roads managed by turnpike trusts snaked their ordered way across the land. Cobbett was repeatedly summoned to court in Bow Street for his refusal to pay tolls in protest. The previous state of the country's roads were by all accounts often awful and we can understand the enthusiasm which with the turnpikes were frequently met. In Sussex the Wealden clay was particularly notorious, its few roads into the interior often almost impassable, villages often isolated, before the new roads. But we can spare a little sympathy perhaps for the turnpikes' discontents. Do we lose something with every gain of innovation, every move to a greater efficiency, each step towards sleepless, relentless mobility as far from our prehistory as can be? Perhaps we are being encouraged at times, and as the lockdowns may have helped remind us, to take a gentler path; to step away, where we can, from frenetic obligations, to appreciate those slow old roads that can speak to heel and hoof, not macadamised surfacing that bears us all the faster, all the further from the people we once knew. Cobbett encouraged travellers to avoid the turnpikes and explore the older trackways, stating that 'those who travel on turnpike roads know nothing of England.'

I woke about six the following morning after a dream initially laden with apparent doom until I found myself on a train with a friend, the carriage all Victoriana and iron, spiralled staircases winding ever further up so it was a wonder, I thought, we fitted under bridges at all. At a session I had forgotten my whistle but a friend had one to hand. As on the train, there was a distinct taste of optimism in the air. I drifted back to sleep until about nine. I thought about an American guy I once knew who was hitching in the 'States and tied his ankle to a motorway barrier one night so he could sleep without falling down the embankment. I could only count my relative blessings.

During the course of the next morning I saw three or four jays, the last almost seeming a sparrow for being so young, hopping off infront of me into woodland as I made my way onwards. The track veered away from the motorway as the morning wore on so that most of the day was surprisingly tranquil and mostly through unpopulated woods. I took wrong turnings twice, both of them easily remedied. As I sat eating lunch after directly climbing a ridge, a sharp but short slope dotted with sprawling oaks to the side of the path, two buzzards glided round a tree further down the hill. Later, as I sat under another huge oak outside some woods, another circled not so very high overhead, giving its wings a friendly-seeming waggle as I adjusted my map. The weather was pleasant and cool with light and high clouds punctuating the sun, perfect for walking, and showing signs of growing warmer.

As was often the case, the chief worry was getting more water. I had an eye on a church where three roads met. But when I circumambulated the building, no tap was forthcoming. I sat in the burgeoning heat, grass growing long and already yellow at the edge of the graveyard, wondering what to do next. At which point I saw a tap standing free some twenty yards away. I filled my bottles, a little surreptitious so as not to alert a groundsman with a mower who was in a state of, or imitating, obliviousness to my presence. I briefly thought a large nearby gravestone was a person, from the corner of my eye, looming golden in the sun. I ate my lunch on a bench by the church and had a brief impression of many people in the field over a low hedge all looking in at me; a curious host.

A wayside marker a little further pointed 48 miles to Farnham and 65 to Canterbury, somewhat discouragingly. I tried not to think about the distance too much, but if I stuck to ten miles a day I reckoned I'd be there in another six days. Ten miles was my general distance for a day's walk for me in those days, with all the gear I was lugging though I could occasionally push it to 15 if I really wanted to. But why be masochistic? The day to Box Hill had been about 15, maybe 17 miles by the time I'd pitched camp. A friend I once walked with had reminded me repeatedly we weren't in the army. I'd waited two hours at the station for him after our agreed time of rendezvous, albeit reading Under Milk Wood so I wasn't too vexed. We made slow headway when we finally set out but when we stopped for lunch he brewed mint tea on a tiny canteen stolen from some motorway café with a little fire of twigs, not wrong that this was no military set up. It felt compensatory.

It was a far cry nonetheless from the yomps in my teens. My father, ex-army, had shown me how to use a compass, up on the nature reserve at the top of hill and I'd used it on those early walks before I'd left home, taking bearings that weren't really necessary to stiles across fields, full of fire with the novelty of sleeping out and the prospect of my girlfriend waiting at a steadily decreasing distance. I certainly never really questioned the martial mind and very nearly could have gone to Sandhurst in the immediately preceding years. Fencing, re-enactments, joining the protests that were not always short of an element of confrontation, however unlooked for, none of it felt particularly contradictory.

But there's big difference between rough and tumble, even dangerous pastimes and actually setting yourself up psychologically and physically against someone in a state of genuine conflict, as I would discover. The army coloured my early life nonetheless, however distinct my father's polished footwear and the trailing laces of my dusty second-hand paraboots might have been. All the same, the rigor of subsequent pilgrimage in Spain would earn his disciplined thoroughness my eventual respect.

I'd walk this route again with a friend a few years later.

He'd made the walk very public via sponsorship and on the first day announced he'd booked us into a hostel in Canterbury in eight days' time, which meant we'd have to pick up the pace. Just for a moment, as it became clear on our first day that this would be no relaxed saunter, resentment bloomed in my blood, before setting off in his wake at a mild canter. But getting a move on for days at a time would turn out to be useful, later. As it was, my dreams were full for weeks afterwards of nothing but our frequent stopping in church porches, homes from home, the only breaks we took amid the miles and miles of frenetic trekking.

I still sometimes wonder how things may have been if I hadn't exposed myself at a young age to the level of drug taking that was so endemic on the protest scene back then, to say nothing of the psychological screwiness it was so easy to encounter and which probably went with the psychedelics. The nineties dripped with drugs of course and in any case an army life might have opened me up to other psychologies difficult to deal with to say nothing of much greater and obvious dangers. All the same, coming off recreational drugs was one of the better moves of my life.

The path emerged from the woods, looking down over a scene so iconically pastoral it almost seemed unlikely. A hollow ran down the towards the somehow diminished-seeming motorway; woods running down the hill alongside and left of the path, the curve of the place a true beauty, the turf soft, hued a little brown, sheep here contented and tranquil. I attempted to resist the urge to stop for a while and take it all in. It was one of those strange moments where the place was so perfect you wanted to be there forever but immediately knew you would have to move on and might as well do sooner before you fell in love. All the same, I must have lingered for awhile.

If it wasn't for my dwindling water I might have camped there but as it was I had my eye on a campsite near the junction of the M25 and M26. My map was old however, borrowed from a friend, and there was no sign of the campsite when I got to where I thought it should be, across flat meadows and the motorways themselves. Short of water in the mounting heat, I walked over a roundabout on an adjacent A-road, past a sprawling, unremarkable looking pub with an indescript frontage of double glazing and down another busy road for a stretch, pushing onto Otford for the night. The last mile across featureless flat fields and across a railway felt a particular stretch after the noise of the roads.

It was here, or at least in the meadows immediately to the north of the village, that Offa, King of Mercia, that one-time rival of Wessex, had fought the Kentish Jutes in an attempt to gain the supremacy of England in 776 AD. Mercia of course was the great Midland kingdom in the Anglo-Saxon period, for hundreds of years a much greater force than Wessex and other kingdoms in the South. It is perhaps not too fanciful to imagine that some of the roots of regional distinctions in our culture go back to this time, though Danelaw may have played an equal if not greater part. In fact, Edmund Ironside was meant to have fought and defeated Canute and the Danes here in 1016, who were routed as far as Aylesford. The outcome of the first battle of Otford in 776 is uncertain but it seems likely the Jutes held out against the Mercians for awhile afterwards. Belloc also informs us of 'a doubtful bit of tradition' that the British defeated the Saxons here in the Fifth Century, who also retreated towards Aylesford. Belloc attributes all these battles to the crossing place coinciding with the route defending forces would have taken when facing invasion from the Thames Estuary.

If all these reports of battles made my head swim, notions of a Mercian distinction gave me cause for more agreeable thought. One boundary point between Wessex and Mercia was the Ridgeway that runs up through Wiltshire and forms part of the Berkshire Downs. From Barbury Castle, not far from Uffington and its iconic White Horse, you can look out on the vale spanning north; seemingly limitless lands on the relative flat towards and past a distant Oxford where willow-lined riversides run through the shires. The castle became part of Wessex in the sixth century after the battle of Beranburgh, just to the north, where the Romano British were defeated. Just down the ridge is Liddington Castle, credited by modern scholars as being the site of Badon Hill the century before, where the Romano British, led by Arthur in the stories, defeated the Anglo-Saxon invaders.

The Uffington horse is associated with King Alfred too, as celebrated in G.K. Chesterton's 'Ballad of the White Horse'. The ballad is perhaps one of the last great epic poems of the English language and, true to the form of many ballads, deals with tradition rather than fact. It describes the defeat of the Danes and is concerned with the need for vigilance against corruption in times of peace, reflected in the ritual act of scouring the hill figure of weeds. The ballad was famous for decades with its call to courage in the face of overwhelming odds; 'the joy without a cause' offering 'nought for your comfort'. It inspired columnists in World War Two and gave succour to soldiers in both World Wars who often carried copies with them to the respective fronts.

I'd dreamt I met friends from Nottingham at Barbury once. We were in a wood, hornbeam by the looks of it and somehow almost rectangular like some kind of outgrown hall. There was a sense of liminality, of places and territory meeting and crossing over, the atmosphere lustred like a very humid day, a sense of things being as real if not more so than my waking life. It was a kind of rapprochement, a meeting of minds, a sense that even in these southern counties I was never alone.

Once I had a dream there should be a gathering there though when I subsequently tried to instigate one in the waking world nothing went right. Vehicles broke down, a friend who promised a scouting mission didn't come through. Nonetheless, someone with a campervan appeared at the last minute and a few of us piled in. A few friends were to be found on the ramparts when we eventually got there and we subsequently made our way off a hilltop to avoid the warden, making our way along a footpath down the road a little to light a fire. As I walked through the dark with a friend something loomed infront of us; a cow or a horse I thought for a moment but it turned out to be a large upright sarsen. My friend ran his hands over it, said it was inscribed, though I thought he was making it up at first, and began to read the words by sparking his lighter repeatedly.

'It is eternity now,

I am in the midst of it.

It is about me in the sunshine.'

Another plaque on the other side of the stone read:

'Still to find and still to follow.

Joy in every hill and hollow.

Company in solitude.'

It turned out to be a memorial to the great Victorian natural historian Richard Jeffries and his near contemporary Alfred Williams, men I had been unaware of until then. The sarsen stone had once sat atop the hilltop but had been moved at some stage, apparently to avoid vandalism. In 'Wildlife in a Southern County' Jeffries writes vividly of Barbury and the Downs here. He writes at length of summer days looking out over the vale from the fort, a little wind cooling him as he watched the hawks and butterflies, no sense at all of any kind of rush. In particular he writes of the rooks in the wood adjacent to the earthworks which still can be seen and heard today. He describes the rook parliaments...

'...an assemblage of hundreds of republics. We know how free states indulge in speech with their parliaments and congresses and senates, their public meetings, and so forth : here are a hundred such nations, all with perfect liberty of tongue, holding forth unsparingly... The din is wonderful – each republic as its forces arrive adding to the noise... In spring each tribe has its special district, its own canton and city, its own trees away in the meadows.'

He illustrates the daily migrations of the rooks; flying off to their territories in steadily diminishing bands as they disperse then returning and converging gradually to one great mass in the evening with such regularity the country people could set their watches by their flight. It couldn't help remind me of the clan of rooks in the woods of Nottingham, who my friends use to watch bowling over and over through the sky above the village green. It all spoke of belonging, the immanence of nature, a collective resonance with my friends and the wildlife they knew they were not separate from. Perhaps above all, in writing of the rooks and birds in general, Jeffries credited them with an intelligence and even culture far beyond what is normally ascribed;

'I think that neither considerations of food, water, shelter, nor convenience are always the determining factors in the choice made by birds of the spots they frequent ; for I have seen many cases in which all of these were evidently quite put on side. Birds to ordinary observation seem so unfettered, to live so entirely without rhyme or reason, that it is difficult to convey the idea that the precise contrary is really the case.'

The rooks at Barbury were out in force when I paid the place a visit, their choruses rolling over and over each other, a tumult of beating wings and vocalisation as they found respective places in the trees. I was reminded of this to hear them that time by the shepherds hut, with a feeling of familiarity. Time, just like distance, it felt can fold in on themselves, carry us back to that which is most precious to our hearts. I felt in both places to be somehow close to my brothers and sisters, to unlikely clans even if the rooks themselves were somehow still at one remove, their voices carrying knowledge of the liminal. But I couldn't shake the feeling of being at home, the cries like those of old ambassadors between the human realm and other kingdoms, hidden from our view.

Back in the meadows before Otford, I was overtaken by three late middle-aged walkers, all with daypacks and generic hiking outfits. They said they were just out for the day and not going far but I had the feeling they were clandestine pilgrims, not wanting to let on. On the outskirts of the village, through an indescript estate of nineteen thirties redbrick that could have been anywhere in the country, a newsagent had just closed, banishing the prospect of immediately quenching my thirst. I could feel the beginnings of a blister on my little toe, the one that had played up before, more than a little concerning.

Otford was full of boutique-type shops and timber framed houses, centred around a green surrounded by roads but with a small pond, men outside a pub I passed who may or may not have cast aspersions about the size of my rucksack. I saw the secret pilgrims again in the atmospheric interior of The Bull on the high street, a rambling pub, done out quite modern with leather seating and stripey carpets but clearly old with all the low ceilings and beams. The posse of possible pilgrims were friendly up to a very firm point and I left them to it and had a meal in the garden, sat on a square, black wicker chair underneath an awning, served by unusually enthusiastic staff. I made my way over the river, the watershed of so much fighting, and up the hill in the twilight.

It was a steep climb up to Otford Mount, intimidating-looking on the map at the end of the day with all the contours, up a little path under trees and past back gardens. I caught my breath on a bench near the top where someone had graffitied 'SPOOKS' vertically in purple paint on a concrete post. Which kind of spooks were being referred was not obvious, but the place felt full of the kind of atmosphere so redolent at Chantries Wood. I made my way past a tree-lined meadow up on the flat and pitched up, in mildly drunken exhaustion, right by a footpath in some woods near a junction of a relatively quiet road.

Sleeping near crossroads is generally not highly recommended. Noises I couldn't quite place disturbed my sleep, as if the woods themselves were restless. I woke at three and thought I might not sleep again but somehow managed to drift off. It was a by-now-not-unusual concern over insomnia, characterised by hours in the dark of my tent, wondering if any given trip was over. I'd taken one of the heavy sleepers and woke again later, kicking off at a sense of something wrong or annoying, literally kicking the roof of the tent's tiny frame with both feet with such force I felt lucky I hadn't damaged it.

I dreamed of a ghoulish middle-aged woman with short curly hair, frightening but not unfriendly, a suicide perhaps, at the crossroads, pointing the way to Canterbury, imploring and encouraging at once. Before dawn I thought I could hear children laughing outside my tent, vivid and real, a thing I'd only heard once before in some coppiced woods at a camp in Newbury when I was sharing a tent just off route. Were these the Jamiroquai of legend? At least, that's what I thought the shaman had described them as. The shaman in question, self-styled perhaps, was a figure from those days who liked to go clubbing in his climbing harness. Had I misheard him? Given that I couldn't find any reference to this name despite the very obvious modern band, it's likely he meant the Taliloquay, North American equivalents of our 'Little People'. There was a real feel of lingering magic and joy upon waking. I struck my camp, such as it was, and carried on, keener than ever to be on my way.

Clarendon

Such things were as far away as can be from a Sunday morning in October 1163, when a piece of high theatre was being enacted in Westminster Abbey. The body of Edward the Confessor, that most saintly of Anglo-Saxon kings, was being moved within the abbey from a tomb to a shrine, now above ground, following his recent canonisation. The new saint's remains were wrapped in silk before being processed around the abbey's cloisters in a wooden coffin, borne on the shoulders of Henry and half a dozen notable barons. It was a clear honouring of Henry's Saxon connections as well as a statement that the monarchy was fit to preside over the English Church. The archbishop should have played a key role in the service, but Becket was deliberately sidelined, effectively snubbed, the role of master of ceremonies going to the Abbot of Westminster instead.

Later, the abbey would be the scene of the first of exchanges where the king and Becket's contest for supremacy in the courts would escalate and crystalise the already existing enmity. The exchanges would set the men ever more against one another and define the parameters of the coming conflict. With the bishopric and even the papacy increasingly sucked in, Becket would look antagonistic and compromised by turns. In his mind at least it would become not just a battle for the soul of the English church, but that of Christianity itself, Henry increasingly cast in his eyes as more than just a political tyrant. Whether pushed to it or not, it would define Becket's view of both Henry and himself, setting the stage for everything that would eventually come to pass.

It began in the abbey's council chamber. With Becket

no doubt still smarting from the earlier snub of the ceremony, Henry demanded criminous clerks be judged by secular courts. Becket, after retiring to consult with his colleagues responded with the words; 'God will not judge twice for the same offence'. It was more of a theological than a legal argument. Henry ordered the bishops' loyalty to which the archbishop replied 'Yes, in every way – saving our order.'

To the control-freak monarch, it was a red rag. 'Poison lurks in that phrase… You shall not say anything of "saving our order", … it is nothing more than sophistry.' The king stormed out of the chamber. The next day he ordered the surrender of all castles and estates in Becket's possession and removed Prince Henry from the archbishop's household where, in a gesture of now vanished respect and fraternity, he had been sent for education.

The monarch subsequently summoned Becket to a meeting at Northampton. But Thomas was denied entry to the town, the king stating it was already full of his courtiers and their retainers. According to the hagiographers, when the two men did approach each other, both their horses reared and they had to change steeds. 'Have I not raised you from a poor and lowly station to the pinnacle of rank and honour?' asked Henry when they came to talk. When he later posed the question as to whether Thomas was not the son of one of his villeins Becket, not very humbly, replied 'I am not sprung from royal ancestors, but neither was St Peter, the prince of the Apostles, to whom the Lord deigned to give the keys of the kingdom of heaven and the primacy of the whole Church.'

'True,' replied a caustic Henry, 'but he died for his Lord.'

'And I will die for my Lord when the time comes… I trust and rely on God, for cursed is the man that puts his hope in man,' responded Becket. He went on to add, perhaps in an

132

attempt at placation, 'I answer, as I did before, that I am ready to please and honour you saving my order.' An angry Henry demanded the phrase be dropped altogether. When Becket refused the two spurred their horses and parted.

Did Becket, even at this stage, think of himself as a soon-to-be martyr? Was his perspective coloured by an over-weaning self-regard? Or did he simply have the measure of his foe? It was all another sign perhaps of his zealousness in his new position, that niggling root of insecurity. Did he aspire even then for sainthood, or was he compelled by a sense of innate destiny? Did he somehow know what lay in store, even as he seemed to will it on? In Becket's mind, the Christian Faith itself was now in danger, Henry looming in his mind as more than a temporal foe. Henry, in his eyes, apparently sought justice but would abandon or twist the law whenever it suited him. At one point Becket proclaimed to a prelate sent to placate him; 'Far be it that I buy back the favour of an earthly king through such a bargain!'

The two sides lobbied the papacy. The pope, pleased with Thomas in some respects but also sensing he was becoming something of an embarrassment, advised the archbishop to lie low. Becket was told Henry had agreed to a verbal pledge of fealty to his 'ancestral customs' - that favourite phrase of the king's - that harked back once again to the apparent peace and security of his grandfather's reign. All Becket had to do, the one little, solitary thing was drop his own cherished mantra 'saving my order'.

After a meeting at Woodstock Becket vowed to observe the customs and obey the king. Henry responded to this climb down by declaring a new council for January 1164

133

where every important figure in the land could hear Becket's words of submission. The king then rode away to spend a lavish Christmas - pointedly - at one of the castles freshly sequestered from his former chancellor. Becket prepared a route of escape for potential exile.

Pope Alexander knew he needed Henry's favour to keep the Holy Roman Emperor, Frederick Barbarossa - who Henry got on well with - on board. Becket's friend John of Salisbury, who had started to prepare a haven for Becket abroad reported he'd heard it said that 'the pope will visit Canterbury Cathedral to knock your candlestick out of its place.' Sensing Henry would never acknowledge a set of values other than his own, Becket would be moved to play the rebel - an impulse familiar from his teens - to become, as his friend John put it, 'the defender of liberty' itself.

+ + +

The new council would take place at the palace of Clarendon near Winchester. Henry opened proceedings by asking Becket to redeem his promise made at Woodstock. Becket, smelling a trap, sought the advice of the bishops but they were reluctant to change their 'saving our order' replies made at the council at Westminster Abbey when individually quizzed by the petulant king. They had followed Becket's lead in this and felt he had painted them into a corner and that now it was incumbent on him to lead them out. Henry apparently had them locked up for two days in an effort to focus their attention. Most were unbowed.

Henry raged he would execute or castrate those who resisted him and sent in a cohort of heavies to threaten the bishops and, later, a cohort of Knights Templar to try and more softly persuade them. The knights staked their eternal

134

salvation on Henry's honesty, stating if Becket relented the bishops would never hear more of the detested 'customs'. Becket subsequently unconditionally submitted; the bishops forced to follow his example.

At this point Henry broke his vow to accept a verbal assent, insisting that everything be put into writing. He produced a cleverly constructed document exploiting every loophole and ambiguity in canon law and feudal custom, effectively doing away with the Church's jurisdiction. If agreed, it would represent total submission.

The document accepted, Becket was effectively undone. He lamented on the return journey "I begin to see that it is through me, and because of my sins, that the English Church is reduced to slavery." His servants muttered against him, his cross-bearer asking "What virtue is left to a man who has betrayed his conscience and his reputation?" Becket fasted, did penance and wore sackcloth, suspending himself from saying Mass. A letter from the pope urged him "not in any way to observe your promise, but rather take care to revoke it…"

Bitter communications flew between England and Rome. The pope urged Becket to keep a low profile. Henry's youngest brother William died, apparently pining away for the love of his would-be bride that Becket had formerly forbidden him marrying, on the grounds of the couple being third cousins. It would only compound Henry's hatred for the archbishop. Becket made further plans to secure a place of exile.

At this point he made some unsuccessful attempts to cross the Channel. During the first the sailors on the ship he hired, when some way out to sea, mutinied, fearing Henry's wrath, and they put back in port. Henry's men came to confiscate his goods after he had returned, having heard of his flight, but were thrown into confusion and backed off when Becket appeared.

Fearing a papal interdict on England if Becket ran to the pope, Henry entertained him at Woodstock with studied courtesy. "So my lord… " he enquired, "…you wish to leave my kingdom: I suppose it is not large enough to hold both of us?" Henry was simply waiting to strike, seeking to avoid a confrontation with the pope, and soon summoned Becket to court over a dispute over a case study of the 'ancestral customs'. When Thomas refused to respond, Henry issued a fresh summons at Northampton, intending to humble and break the archbishop. His officials began to scour Becket's records during his time as chancellor, looking for evidence of misdemeanours. Becket was more convinced than ever of Henry's tyrannous streak.

The trial began at Northampton Castle in October 1164. If Becket refused again to submit, and to do so in a legally binding form, Henry intended to try him for treason. When Becket offered the customary kiss of peace on greeting, Henry refused him, later demanding Becket be forfeited all his movable property. The king claimed that, as much of his wealth was now written off, Becket must find sureties or face incarceration. He demanded Becket accounted for all revenues as chancellor, which, as Thomas argued, had not been mentioned in writ of summons.

When the bishops tried to mediate, Henry locked them up again to "hurry along their deliberations". Some of them advised Becket to resign the archbishopric. Others urged him to stand firm. On Sunday the court adjourned. Becket's colitis flared and he was unable to ride to the castle the following day. Henry suspected foul play. A rumour flew around he wanted Becket dead or in a dungeon. The bishops told Becket that Henry now meant to try him as a traitor and urged him again to resign. Becket argued it wasn't his fate at stake but that of the entire Church. For him, the time had come to make a stand.

Prohibiting the bishops from taking part in any

judgement against him, Becket urged excommunication for any secular men that laid their hands on him. "Know this, that although the world rages, the enemy rises, the body quivers and the flesh is weak, I shall, God willing, never give in shamefully or commit the offence of abandoning the flock that is entrusted to me."

The appeal to the bishops effectively made Becket a pariah. The church men left hurriedly for the castle. Provocatively donning the pallium – a kind of ecclesiastical mantle and the ultimate symbol of his office - Becket said mass at a nearby church, the special mass used on St Stephen's Day in honour of that first Christian martyr. The battle was about to begin in earnest.

Dismounting in the castle-yard, Becket took his archiepiscopal cross, holding it before him as if armed and marched towards the great hall. Some thought he intended to excommunicate Henry and perhaps this was true as the king was subsequently unwilling to confront Becket head on while he held this religious instrument. While still outside, a follower of the king's tried to seize it, an unseemly fracas ensuing.

The bishops, some in tears, urged Thomas to repeal the prohibition on their judgement. The archbishop refused to compromise; hadn't the 'customs' been condemned by the pope as obnoxious?

Deputations scurried between the antechamber Becket now sat in and the king's chamber. Becket gave a defiant speech in his own defence, forbidding the bishops to judge him, a speech some considered blasphemous. Roger of Pont l'Eveque, archbishop of York and Becket's great rival, descended the stairs and a cross-off ensued, so that it look like the two ecclesiastical giants might come to blows before Hilary of Chichester intervened, turning on Becket, accusing him of starting all the trouble at Clarendon when he urged the bishops to follow his lead before changing tack. Becket stated that no one was beholden to an oath that ought not to have been made in the first place.

The suggestion was made that if Henry excused the bishops from passing judgement on Becket, they would launch an appeal to the pope against their archbishop, asking him to be deposed. Henry agreed. To add further legitimacy to proceedings he asked all the knights and sheriffs of the shires to sit with the barons in casting judgement. The sources do not tell us what the sentence was but Becket was certainly condemned, most probably to life imprisonment.

Becket sat awaiting the announcement. But the king's man wavered and Thomas interrupted, forbidding anyone there to judge him. When it was clear he was about to be sentenced he jumped up, raising his cross on high. "It is not for you to judge your archbishop for a crime!" he cried. Barons shouted "perjurer" and "traitor". A second, also ham-fisted, attempt was made to deliver the sentence. Hilary of Chichester said that treason was clear and that Becket hear the pronouncement but Becket, his cross before him, made for the door. Others joined in the cry against him as he stumbled over firewood in the great hall. "If only I were a knight, my own fist would give you the lie," he shouted back.

Jumping onto his horse outside, a follower joined him in the saddle. The gates of the outer bailey were still locked but a bunch of keys were hanging from the wall – the porter absent, possibly beating a boy. Becket and his clerks escaped through the town, an admiring crowd following his wake, cheering him on; a people's hero who had resisted a tyrant.

Back at the nearby priory where he was staying, Becket sent a message to the king asking for safe conduct to Canterbury. Henry replied that a decision on this this would be made the next day. Becket said he would spend the night in prayer at the priory chapel, the monks making up a bed for him behind the altar. Pretending to be asleep, he left an hour before dawn, disguised as a lay brother with three companions, heavy rain masking the sound of the hooves of his horse. They knew the north gate of the town was unguarded. When a bishop enquired at the priory after Becket later that morning he was told, "He is doing rather well, since he left late last night in a hurry and no one knows where he is gone." Henry, on hearing the news, in the vein of a comedy villain, simply said "We've not finished with this wretched fellow yet."

The Crossing

I spent the morning walking gorgeous stretches on the ridge with mature trees and pasture spanning out to the south, views of the opposite ridge. Could that be where I'd camped under the beeches not so very long ago? Or was that further off? And could I catch sight of the South Downs still this far east? A pair of shire horses, piebald and white, stood placid and indifferent as I passed along grassland dotted with oaks. Later, horses with visors to keep off the flies, friendly and wary at once. It was a time of woods and fields and steady going.

I dropped from the ridge and walked along a flat path at its foot. Belloc believed this stretch was a kind of model for the 'Old Road's' character. He was referring entirely to the lower track, the Pilgrims' Way as marked on the map, rather than the route of the North Downs Way up on the ridge. The original way, if we accept the premise of its existence at all, probably took the lower road all the way from Otford, skirting closer to the village of Kemsing, the North Downs Way only joining this older route at the point it becomes unmetalled though in earlier times of course there would have been no such distinction.

Many modern country lanes are sole survivors of the process of tarmacking the road. Whereas perhaps several lanes once provided steady going, with the advent of covering the surface in steaming tar; the modern means of 'macadamising' (named for John London McAdam, surfacer extraordinaire of turnpikes back in the day), many minor routes fell into complete disuse. There were originally three 'Great North Roads' and turnpikes themselves, by encouraging some main routes, caused others to be abandoned. In the Nineteen Thirties, no council could afford to tar all its routes, leading to gaps to be found in the roadways in more ancient parts of our landscape. The tar then was simultaneously the preserver and destroyer of old paths. The Pilgrims' Way at this point owes its very existence to its use.

Along the 'Way here can be found the fabled 'Kemsing milestone'. Antiquarians have made much of this early Eighteenth Century waymarking rock as it predates the turnpike down in the valley and thereby proves the use of the route in the Seventeenth Century - providing tenability of the theory of its use medieval times. The milestone another reminder of the tenuous nature of proof of the pilgrimage route; its importance a reflection of the lack of hard evidence elsewhere.

Belloc too had his theories. The flat path would become a characteristic of the 'Way further on and may have predated the villages it frequently skirts. It would have begun, he argued, as the main route through the area, then became an alternate way supplemented by a valley road before finally becoming a largely unused path virtually destroyed by the more modern highway below it. Today we can add a further detail; the motorways so blue on the map further down into the valley.

A road separate from the villages, if only by a little way, would not be without its advantages. In the event of crime, strangers and vagrants could often be blamed, helping account for the legislation in the Middle Ages to try and prevent lower classes from travelling. This could reflect labour shortages as well as attempts to discourage vagabonds. At any rate, as those who were meant to be locked to the land were often supposed to carry their letter of dispensation if travelling, a route that skirted conurbations held an extra boon for those travelling sans documentation. To boot, ancient trackways could sometimes be safer considering what might lie in wait along more modern roads. And they avoided the tolls of the turnpikes.

Otford and Wrotham were the sites of great ecclesiastical palaces, along with Maidstone and Charing, Boxley and Hollingbourne. "All these things had gone utterly, the countryside we were treading held their principle and silent memorials," lamented Belloc. With something of an intuitive approach to history and Roman Catholic, Belloc felt the loss of the monasteries along the route during the Reformation more keenly than most. He also believed Henry VIII may have taken this route from Otford on the way to that great extravaganza of diplomatic showmanship, the Field of the Cloth of Gold. William the Conqueror (or 'the Bastard' to give him his other appellation) and invading Romans may have also done the same, albeit travelling the other way.

To Belloc's frame of mind, these things happened not so long ago, or he felt at least their memory was somehow kept fresh. But Belloc sometimes had a flexible approach to the past, citing at one stage that history "is a matter of flair rather than facts." Still, there was no doubt that Henry's break from Rome still smarted. "The catastrophe is scarred over the history of the countryside like the old mark of a wound… I know of no district in England where the heavy, gross and tortured face of Henry in his decline haunts one more. Sacredness is twofold – of pleasure and pain and this, the sacred end of our oldest travel, suffered in proportion to its sanctity."

The Friaries and Abbeys of the Middle Ages were powerhouses of social welfare and education and it was paradoxical that the Reformation which swept so many of them away was a reaction to indulgences, perceived and real, of a monastic life that had been subject to so many minor reformations of their own. Benedictines, Carthusians, Cistercians, Franciscans, Dominicans, they were all

142

movements to strip away creeping luxuries of monastic life, seeking to return them to an ascetic purity the Desert Fathers in their caves in North Africa would have approved of.

When Christianity, which had hitherto been a persecuted minority cult, became adopted by Emperor Constantine in particular and the larger Roman world in general in the Fourth Century, some followers chose to withdraw from this sudden populism. The Desert Fathers were perhaps the most obvious manifestation of this. Hermits like Anthony of Egypt were followed by communal monastics, foregoing property and money and subjecting themselves to a harsh ascetic that could border on the incredible if admittedly sometimes extreme. Simon of Stylites lived up a pillar for years, others lived in trees or walled themselves into enclosures, others still wore clothes made of thorns. But however strange some of that may seem to us, they were trying to live closer to God and to imitate the sufferings of Christ. The monasteries of North Africa still exist and are keystones of a fierce asceticism that continue to inspire many today.

Back in Europe, in the run up to the Reformation, the indulgences of flesh among monastics did exist, however hyped for political ends. Sometimes this was due to monasteries and convents sheltering wayward children of the rich who were keen to maintain an extravagant lifestyle and weren't exactly committed to a pious life. One example of this was the interruption of mass by nuns returning from the hunt though other charges are more serious. There is no doubt however that the monasteries themselves, despite their members' vows of poverty could become quite rich on the back of efficient farming and virtually free labour. But an equally great issue was the other Indulgences of the Catholic Church – whereby prayers could be bought to redeem any sin. This was a veritable cash cow as was the trade in portions of relics of Saints and was reprehensible for the implication you could buy your way to salvation, however heinous your deeds, if not actually subject to law.

All the same, the decimating effect of the Reformation on English social and religious life cannot be understated; 3000 monasteries were closed between 1536 and 1539 and, beyond the well-attested discontentment with the lack of adherence to chastity and poverty, a very real hunger for land and riches among the Reformation's beneficiaries also cannot be denied. We're encouraged now to see the likes of Thomas Cromwell as a kind of modern-minded everyman. But the scale and speed of dissolution and destruction tells a far harder story to hear.

It's particularly pertinent to me as, like Belloc, I come from a Roman Catholic family – a recusant remnant of this older brand of the faith. Throughout the Sixteenth and Seventeenth Centuries ancestors of mine from the Lancashire, Yorkshire borders had kept practising Catholicism despite the prospect of fines and very visceral persecution. I was reared on a diet of historical novels depicting life at this time, where priests themselves were the smuggled contraband and penalties were fierce. It was a factor in my continued church going as a teenager – shouldn't I keep the tradition up after all those earlier sacrifices? At the best of times, English Roman Catholics after the Reformation have been thin on the ground so there was a sense of a lineage to preserve.

The schism between Catholicism and Protestantism is a fault line which has divided the nation's religious life and politics right up to the Jacobite rebellions. It's an example, if one were needed, of religious division fuelling violence and antipathy, another black mark in religion's own book, giving fuel to those who'd argue for a move away from organised religion altogether. At such times as these for the world, it's as important as ever that we respect one another's differences, that we are not beholden to dogma or let

144

divisions blind us to the original spirit and message of the prophets. It has been speculated that Shakespeare came from a Catholic family and that Romeo and Juliet, with its rival factions, came from a desire to articulate the power of love amid times of partition. For when we strip away dividing lines we're all of us within the fold of a shared humanity, whether we're Shia or Sunni, Protestant, Catholic, Druid, Buddhist or choose not to keep a religion at all.

There are more modern echoes of monastic sensibility. My dreams of castles and cathedrals were sometimes augmented by those of old colleges, including one dream where I toured the ancient schools of Sussex in the holidays by bus. Inside one, past the stone walls of a courtyard, was a boy with a red and yellow scarf, glasses, welcoming me to an indoor party, like a festival, festooned with drapes and disused parachutes, the people there kindly and wise. There was a sense of sudden fellowship, an embarkation into a kind of new world that was at once homely and ancient.

I reached Wrotham a little earlier than planned. Like Otford and Kemsing before it, Wrotham is a spring-line village in the Vale of Holmesdale. The path, dusty in the rising morning heat, led me along to the north of the houses before I dropped down into the conurbation, small though it was, to look for water. A pub on the map was now a private house, tantalising, so I doubled back to try the tap of a spectacularly ugly and grimly dispositioned public toilet cubicle which was, probably quite fortunately, closed. So I turned again and headed for the Rose and Crown, drinking a coffee on a sun-soaked table outside while an unopened bar of chocolate from the adjacent newsagent steadily melted before me.

In need of more refreshment and escaping the heat, I

145

braved the cool interior, packed, for some reason, with pensioners in their sixties and seventies, starting early. I was left unmolested as I drank an apple juice from a stemmed glass, agreeing with the elderly barmaid that it wasn't quite right that non-alcoholic drinks were so expensive. In the parish newsletter there was a piece about folk traditions in Malaysia; pertinent as tourists had recently, according to the locals there, angered the spirit of a holy mountain and triggered an earthquake on account of their being half naked. Amongst other tips I was advised not to point unless it be with bent second and middle fingers and to only dig graves with a loose-handled spade so that the connection between the living and the dead is not too strong; more relevant than it might have otherwise been after my night at the crossroads.

The pensioners seemed friendly and somehow lit up in a way that had to be accounted for by more than just the early drinking. Relaxed communal banter bounced around and they all felt friendly and sound, a face of this country I hadn't expected down south. One of them talked about speaking Spanish and I felt halfway there just to be in that place. I simultaneously greeted and bid farewell to a friendly old gent as I left, headed back to the track feeling buoyed, optimistic.

The path led over the M20 immediately outside the village, via an A-road on a bridge. Cars slipped by below, surreal and abrasive through the dusty mesh of the bridge's metal fencing. Beyond, where the path again resumed along a bridleway, the view opened up to the east. Belloc had written here that he and his companion "saw before us the whole valley of the Medway, the great flats and distant river and the further hills… a view of astonishing effect," and that "far off, miles and miles away, the hills continued their interminable line."

The day's walk before me certainly marked an important stage of the journey with the crossing of the Medway. The complication was that the North Downs Way looped way up to the north to cross the river at Rochester before returning back, via a similar detour, to roughly opposite in the valley to where it left off. It would easily add a whole extra day's walk. There was a crossing further south, at Alresford, but the route was protracted, involved negotiating many little paths and trekking through the uninviting-sounding conurbation of Snodland.

It was not a new dilemma. Rochester was clearly an established crossing point – there'd been a bridge there in Roman times. There was another a bridge there from about 960 and we know there was one in the Thirteenth Century as its collapse was recorded in 1281. A stone bridge was built a century later. Cartwright believed that pilgrims crossing here would have carried on, as would have those travelling through Rochester to Canterbury from London, along Watling Street, now the A2. It's a theory subscribed to by other, more modern and more factually reliable pilgrimist writers.

There were four other potential crossing points for medieval travellers further south, upstream, Snodland and Aylesford being just two. On my map though the only bridge standing was at Alresford and I had, back at home, planned out a route there, swayed in no small part by various barrows that were circled in biro on my OS map. I'd borrowed half my maps for the journey from an antiquarian tree-surgeon friend and I felt I owed it to him to make a detour to some of these places which he clearly thought so worthy of a visit. The archaeology forms a part of the story of the crossing here with barrows, stones and cairns on both sides of the river bearing out the Old Road's primacy. There had been plenty of prehistoric finds in a line between where I now stood and the hills rising up so tranquil and blue on the far side of the river; Mesolithic flints, Neolithic axes from rock heads, worked gold bracelets and of course the barrows close to hand.

The nearest of these was down a swift succession of small lanes and over fields past an isolated church, the land behind it somewhat overgrown and thistle-clad, confusing. I'd left the North Downs Way now so I had to define my route from a few plastic footpath circles on extremely weather-worn wood, the path scrappy and indeterminate but the fields in full flight of the summer. Soon I was met by an isolated wall of terraced housing, twenties-style, almost sentinel, broken only in the middle by a little gravel avenue to let me pass.

Coldrum Long Barrow, when I found it, was just off the path and flanked by beeches which seemed to have been there almost as long as the barrow itself. On the approach, I could hear faint ringing, bell-like, so that I expected to find a collared dog upon arrival. But it turned out to be mini windchimes on the cloutie-festooned tree; little scraps of cloth tied onto branches as prayers. Large upright boulders marked the entrance to the barrow by the path while another path led up round the back to the tree, also encrusted with various runes carved into the bark.

The whole effect was one of outright enchantment, the windchimes, new age for sure, somehow felt appropriate, faerie-like, and I sat in the crook of the tree for what felt like a very long time. The grass on the top of the barrow, flanked by smaller but still very sizeable grey stones, was wearing a little thin and chestnut rail fencing had been put up which hadn't stopped interlopers, judging by the runnels of bare earth between the posts. Various offerings were in evidence; flowers and feathers and a large chunk of honeycomb. For my part, I unwrapped a hemp energy bar and left it there on the sun-soaked green. A snack for a fox if nobody else.

Coldrum Stones, as the barrow is also known, is part of a rich archaeology in the Medway Valley, with sarsen outcrops occurring on the other side of the river that were readily used in the construction of various burial mounds. The area contains the highest density of chambered tombs, or their remnants, in the South East outside Salisbury Plain. This all points to both a history of sanctity in the area and the likely importance of the North Downs ridge as a thoroughfare in prehistory. In particular it reinforces the case that the route I was taking over the river has an ancient precedent.

Long barrows like this are iconic of the Neolithic, when farming first arrived. No one knows for sure their purpose but the discovery of contemporary bones in the chambers, which were eventually often sealed in, makes their use as having some kind of funerary function highly likely. As with other structures of the time they must have been the product of some kind of community working together and demonstrate the area held a continued relevance to them over several if not many generations. The construction of megalithic tombs in the British Isles continued for some four hundred years. Coldrum Long Barrow probably dates from the fourth millennium BC.

I had the distinct sense the barrow, or attendant spirits, were somehow urging me on, willing me to do better in all I had undertaken. I could only pray and try and renew my endeavours. I felt the place needed treating with the utmost respect and did not want to outstay my welcome. Clearly, as a place of the dead, the place could only have been sanctified. It wasn't a question of idolising stones but of honouring every generation past. I left feeling more than ever that our lives are, or will be, subject to scrutiny, that our forefathers and mothers are never so very far away and that we must always strive to live our lives with honour. Places like Coldrum Stones offer us a glimpse into, or meeting point between our world and the next. Whether we conceive of that as Heaven or a Celtic Otherworld or anything else is arguably besides the point. It's sure to elude any intellectual expectations.

A little further on were some woods I was planning to camp in. I found a suitable place far enough away from the track; flat and not too visible and I sat under a beech feeling pleased with myself. But I hadn't even had my map out long before a cloud of mosquitos descended, perhaps an effect of the sodden and low-lying earth and I shouldered my rucksack to beat a retreat. I tramped around the woods to find another place but each time the mozzies appeared, as if hive-like homing devices and I carried on down the path till I was out of the woods to hide my bag in the undergrowth and seek out some more of the barrows encircled on the map.

I headed down through another field of flax, all greenish and marginally purple, strange in the afternoon light, like I was wading through a shallow and alien sea. Through a sandy underpass and past some kind of sand quarry, I was soon walking down a little path so thick with brambles I thought about turning back and feared for the integrity of my one good cotton, already-torn shirt.

Over the motorway via a little lane on a bridge and I found myself in the village of Addington, peaceful with its tiny little green. The tombs however were barred by a gate that said visits were by appointment only, with a number to call. It felt a bit presumptuous to expect to be admitted there and then and I retraced my steps to the village green, though stopping to admire some sarsens over a fence that were covered in copious green and yellow lichen, with a smell that reminded me of childhood holidays in western Ireland, where the bogs were ubiquitous and beguiling in the intermittent sun.

I sat on an also-licheny bench in the churchyard among the more modern graves and memorised a prayer I had found handwritten in the back of a Bible in a church in central Nottingham, on a no less loaded visit several years after those earlier, more fraught experiences. The church was frequented by junkies, praying for their lives and I felt like I retrieved the prayer by the skin of my teeth. It went:

May we be delivered unto Light,

May there be Joy in our hearts,

May we be protected,

May we be dedicated to Truth,

May we be dedicated to God.

I'd been going through songs in my head or singing aloud upon the walk. Without an mp3 player or iPod it was a means to pass the miles and there was something satisfying about belting out verses at the top of your lungs with no one to hear but the birds. Some songs were kind of prayers and I tried to choose those more appropriate to being on a pilgrimage. Warlike songs from the Highlands I thought were best left and a six-verse ballad to the joys of whiskey was right out. It still left me plenty to choose from and it was a chance to properly practise and commit songs to memory away from the oppressive confines of my flat.

Addington was blessed, 'gifted' as the slightly pretentious phrase nowadays is, with 'The Angel'; a large and welcoming establishment that stated in white writing on a beam above the bar; 'In God we trust... everyone else pays cash'. Somebody was talking about the Camino Santiago. I ate a large meal on a table outside looking over the green and got my finances in order via calls to the bank on my not-very-smart phone. Skylarks took to the air as I crossed back over the field of vaguely blue-hued flax. I was pleasantly drunk in a way that was accounted for by something other than just a few beers.

I put up my little tent in the corner of a wheat field, on a large grassy verge that may have formed set aside land. Later, I was glad of my inner mesh window as mobs of mozzies returned. I picked up my Spanish book again. As it grew dark, bats appeared below a low half-moon. A fox called out nearby as I tried sleeping. I took a double dose. I slept in till about nine, struck my minimal camp a little laboriously. Back in the woods as I returned to the route to Snodland, someone had put little twigs in the catches of the metal gates, attempting to record the passage of unwary pedestrians, for reasons unknown but probably to do with a weariness of traffic related to the barrow.

I tramped along through minor roads and footpaths. A man in his fifties on a horse with sunglasses on his hat and long loose hair seemed to wish me well though we didn't stop to talk as his steed seemed temperamental. I turned down 'Master's Lane', passing a garage with a low-slung silver Delorian, thoughts of time travel strangely appropriate here. Across a wheatfield an electric blue dragonfly appeared to lead the way.

Soon I was in the beginnings of some kind of industrial zone, the path running over old tarmac and weeds between wide rough banks of grass with bricks and concrete slabs and various low-level detritus scattered around, a stand of high laburnum strikingly ugly. Eventually I tumbled out onto an A road through a patch of nettles and brambles, resisting the not-very-alluring option of a coffee from a chrome roadside van. But after a long and slightly harrowing stretch of dual carriageway lined with housing, a supermarket obligingly

152

presented itself, cash machine and all and for once I felt grateful for one of their cafes, drank a large and gratifyingly bitter coffee while people around me tucked into unusually greasy-looking fry ups.

My path led me on down the road, past new housing estates, weather-boarded in primary blues in a nod to traditional architecture but no more enticing to spend any time there for that. After various roundabouts I picked my path along a railway line, hemmed in between fences, dusty with trimmed nettles, a massive industrial complex on my right; old paper mills but more like a gas works with huge cylindrical towers, seemingly dormant but leaving an arid taste in my mouth.

Lorry parks loomed next but somehow I found the Aylesford road, a burger van closing for business as I took a little road past the train station, temptation for butties removed but I got a lemonade and was glad for it as I was suddenly staring at the water of the Medway and the heat and humidity was intense, something I'd tried not to notice as I traced my tortuous way through Snodland's strange and grimy heart. The river was broad and brown with a look like it had a steady undertow. Seagulls here were a surprise but we weren't so very far from the Thames Estuary after all and the Medway itself was much broader not so very far downstream. A half-inflated yellow minion from a cartoon film bobbed upon the water. I was covered in sweat.

With the river to my left, the path led on behind a steel rail, raised up on a stone terrace. On the opposite bank, medieval-looking stonework of a Friary presented itself, inviting with many windows and little walkways. The heat was heavy. There was a sense of immanence. I took myself over the stone of what was clearly an ancient bridge, golden and bulwarked and flagged and cobbled underfoot; a true beauty. Unlikely dreams seemed suddenly possible now.

There was a sense of strange familiarity. It was all I could do to keep going.

Blue Bell Hill

On Aylesford's little high street, replete with an old-looking pub and aged timber frames, I got lunch and water from a newsagent and sat on a bench in the shade of a tree while stereos from cars waiting for the traffic lights blared the chorus of the afternoon. Though time was getting on and it would involve walking back in the other direction, it seemed rude not to pay the Friary a visit. 'The Friars', as it is known, was established in Aylesford in 1247, the first Chapter of the Carmelite Order outside the Holy Land. The Order had been established during the previous century on Mount Carmel in Outremer, as the Crusader States were known, that encompassed modern day Israel. The community there was comprised, as essentially most early monasteries were, of hermits choosing a more communal life. The Carmelites became mendicant friars, in that they lived by begging, something they held in common with the Franciscans and Dominicans, also founded in the Thirteenth Century.

The Friars and Carmelites of Aylesford were victims, like so many more, of the Reformation and the place is almost unique as it is one of the few religious houses that have been restored to their original order during the last century, in the intervening years being occupied variously by merchant bankers, scout leaders, Royalists and soldiers in the Second World War. Past the stonework of an elaborate gateway, a long treelined drive led in to the Friary buildings. A huge open-air auditorium presented itself with rows and rows of simple, long pews. A grand stone altar amid monumental arches, with bright, neo-Catholic style murals on the walls around it formed a suitably impressive focal point.

I walked past it, not without a sense of reverential awe, images of mass pilgrimage coming to mind. A little further, a medieval-looking courtyard presented itself, enclosed by stone buildings that could have been alms houses or other accommodation and I sat beneath a canvas shade outside a great hall or refectory - as it turned out, this is one of the finest surviving medieval courtyards in the country and the hall itself dates from the Thirteenth Century. A brief look inside had revealed long tables and benches and the place looked like it could fit several hundred people, at a push. Paintings of medieval scenes decked the walls; stylised and modernised like something from the thirties but still quite fitting for the theme. Kings and monks and pilgrims with old-style ships upon simultaneously wild and regularised waves vied for attention with scrolls of Latin script beneath them all. A large gallery loomed overhead, like some kind of ancient library. Back outside, a passing young monk blessed me as I sneezed.

Once refreshed, I made my way back to the open-air auditorium and entered a little side chapel to pray. The hushed interior was carpeted, the air stiff and close and a little oppressive, as though the heating was still on. A man entered after me and sat directly behind me, his heavy breathing filling the air. I couldn't concentrate or really feel at peace, was reminded of any of hundreds of settings from my Catholic youth; the seventies kitsch, the tang of incense, here like air freshener, the bling on the altar, a sense of judgement and my own unworthiness to be in such a place. I wondered if the man behind me was some kind of chaplin, keeping an eye on me. I felt out of place, like this sanctum was too intimate, too closed and was glad to return to the spacious architecture outside. I'm happiest I suppose in a large church or cathedral, it's a scale that seems to suit, as if I was out in the woods. In church as a teenager I conjured up images in my mind's eye of churches with vast walls of glass, looking out on the hills and the trees, minimising the separation between outside and in, a separation that at times for me I've felt acutely, the space of being in the woods making four walls seem restrictive. Perhaps it's an ascetic that can help lead us out of cosy hermetically sealed mentalities. Perhaps half the challenge we face in our daily lives is to help bring the outdoors inside.

I was glad to head back into the space of the outdoor chapel, conceived by a Father Malarchy and Adrian Gilbert Scott after the Friary was bought back by the Carmelites in 1949. Work began on the shrine some ten years later and it was rededicated for worship in 1965, Father Malarchy declaring it "a prayer in stone". Across the spanning nave a larger church, full of modern stained glass in a multitude of blues and reds and purples, was exponentially easier to be in. I lit a candle to join a host of others in little red glass jars and prayed. The murals of the main altar outside; angels in bold reds and golds looked down in a friendly fashion. A voice said I'd done well to get here.

Keen to make haste, I nonetheless stopped in at the gift shop, intending to acquire some kind of cross, no small matter, and delved amid the copious plastic rosaries and bejewelled crucifixes. A T-shaped wooden one I'd seen on sale widely in Spain presented itself and I searched my memory for more information. A Spanish anarchist I was walking with had tried to talk me into getting one but I hadn't considered it important and hadn't even associated it with anything overtly Christian. I'd thought it might actually be pagan or a product of some kind of pagan, Christian fusion, my notions hazy and half-formed. Shops out there had had them in their windows and on little racks by doors, ubiquitous, their prominence beckoning to every passing pilgrim.

The woman at the counter here, after quizzing me on some obscure point of devotional Catholic doctrine that left me non-plussed, said it was from Christianity's earliest days of the faithful and I later learned it was Franciscan, which felt entirely appropriate. We all know St Francis talked and preached to the birds and of his famous prayer "Make me a channel of your Peace…". He's famous too for his Canticle of Brother Sun, composed in his final years after his eyesight had failed him. The canticle expressed his veneration of nature as part of God's Creation, praising 'Sister Moon' as well as 'Brother Sun', 'Brother Wind' and 'Brother Fire', 'Sister Mother Earth'. In another famous story, part of the 'Fioretti' (literally 'Little Flowers'; a collection of legends concerning his life), he tamed and possibly converted a wolf who was terrorising an Italian village. He was canonised a swift two years after his death and remains an icon for environmental consciousness, being made Patron Saint of Ecology in 1979.

But it didn't quite start out like that. Son of a wealthy silk merchant, he was a follower of the Troubadours, fond of fine clothes and profligate with cash. At 20 he was taking part in a military expedition against Assisi's neighbouring town. Most of Assisi's troops were slaughtered and he himself was taken prisoner, spending a year in miserable captivity. During this time he became ill and some say that was the beginning of his spiritual awakening. Two years later however, a time apparently spent partying with as much abandon as ever, he was setting out on campaign again, this time as a knight on the Fourth Crusade.

Resplendent on a fine horse with armour decorated with gold, he boasted as he left that he'd return a prince. But a day out from Assisi he dreamed God told him he had it all wrong and should return home. He acted upon it and was laughed at, humiliated back in his home town, his father furious at the money he had wasted. Francis headed to a cave to a pray, weeping, ostensibly for his sins. He went on to found one of the most instrumental orders in the medieval

Church, still going strong to this day. He even travelled to Outremer where he attained a private audience with the Sultan to try and make peace, which may have been instrumental in the Franciscan Order being able to remain in the Holy Land after the Crusades came to a close.

Back at the Friars, the woman at the counter got in a spin about the right price and as I sought out my money Steve Wright on the radio reported from the Glastonbury festival where the loudest-ever thunder had drowned out the sound from the Pyramid stage. I headed back to the village centre and up what looked on the map like a small country lane. But it was an incredibly busy road without a pavement, hemmed in by hedges and walking along it was fraught and felt dangerous. I was determined to stick with it though for the various stones at its end, I owed it to my antiquarian friend, his biro circles goading me on despite there barely being space to get off the road with every passing vehicle.

I took in a seemingly unordered little circle in a tiny hedge-enclosed meadow, briefly paid my respects but was keen to head on with the traffic getting heavier by the minute. Eventually the turning to the path I needed presented itself. At which point a woman in a pink tracksuit with sunglasses presented herself, walking towards me and asking directions as the cars hurtled past. She couldn't make sense of my map so we headed up to a busy crossroads and I was able to point her in the right direction. It was an unlikely encounter and a good thing I'd stopped her taking the road I'd just survived, a brief affirmation of humanity amid the stress.

Then west, through an underpass, semi-octagonal like something from Battlestar Galactica, an electric blue car hurtling through so I had to almost jump out of the way. I walked over a cutting for the Eurotunnel line, the excavations for which had revealed copious archaeology including evidence for a Neolithic longhouse not far from my own crossing point. The trainline was controversial at the time of course, a trail of destruction mitigated by the rich excavations. The arguments for and against high speed lines cannot be compared with Cobbett's somewhat quixotic attitude to turnpikes. The scale of destruction and lasting impact on landscape and habitats are on another level entirely. And yet I've taken the Eurostar as an alternative to cheap flights. But, leaving aside the pros and cons of particular projects, there's a common cord of argument against our modern hypermobility, the sense of displacement it can bring, the sacrifice of that which is immediate and local, the tangible loss of an unquantified intensity. Any piece of infrastructure must be evaluated upon its own merits or lack of them. But all too often, do the results really justify the damage done?

I took a path up through the woods again till I found the Whitehorse Stone, just off the side of the track. A flat sarsen, seemingly on its side, sat in a little grove, bathed in a feeling of untrammelled peace. Somebody had left a little prayer for a loved one tied to a sapling. I briefly payed respects, left another protein bar for good measure. Somehow, I felt very much at home. Making offerings may be seen as a kind of superstitious throwback, but for me it comes from a wish for reverence, if worship is saying too much. You could say these stones were part of God's creation and surely our ancestors were no slouches when it came to their use as any student of the astronomy of stone circles can attest. If we can venerate the great forests in stone our medieval forebears created in the great cathedrals we can admire and value too these sarsens and circles and cairns.

The history of course is a little more fraught. Theodore of Tarsus, Archbishop of Canterbury in the Seventh Century, railed against those frequenting and worshipping stones as did King Canute three hundred years later. But Pope Gregory the Great, a near contemporary of Theodore, wrote the stones should not be destroyed, unless they contained overt pagan imagery but should regarded as part of the natural landscape. Nonetheless in the Thirteen Hundreds, and later, in the Eighteenth and Nineteenth Centuries, the Medway's long barrows were comprehensively trashed. Despite the proximity of Canterbury and Rochester and even the abbeys of Boxley and Malling it is quite possible that non-Christians, even in that late century, were heavily present in the area. The Baltic Crusades, where European pagans were railed against no less ferociously than the Muslims, also under a papal banner, seemed to spur European leaders on and Edwards I and III were apparently heavily involved in this fatwa upon the nation's monuments.

Stones and stone-built barrows were over the centuries variously toppled, buried, cracked with fire, plentiful cold water and heavy hammers and blown up with gunpowder. One technique involved digging adjacent pits until the stones fell into them and then to burn many loads of hay beneath them. People went to extraordinary lengths to hide or destroy or appropriate them. Surviving stones were left in various states of disrepair as curios, objects to be fascinated by or interfered with by burgeoning antiquarians or incorporated into the fabric of nearby buildings such as Addington Church. Only the Ancient Monuments Act of 1882 helped put a stop to this. If Belloc lamented the dissolution of the abbeys here-abouts we can share an equal sentiment at the destruction of these most precious windows into our ancestors' lives.

The White Horse Stone actually inherited its name from another nearby stone (now referred to as the Lower White Horse Stone) which was apparently to be found three hundred metres west of the stone I found myself infront of now. That other stone was destroyed, some think, in the early Nineteenth Century, apparently broken up and thrown into the road and is now to be found beneath the A229, below

161

which the fast, blue car had so nearly dispatched me. The story goes that the standard of the Saxon brothers Hengist and Horsa, a white horse, was flown from the stone during the battle of Aylesford in 455 and was found by or under the stone later on. It is said the story is unlikely to date back before the Seventeenth Century, though others have attributed horse-like physical qualities to the shapes of the stones and it has even been dubbed The Western Sphinx though outright resemblances are not plain to see.

I couldn't help but think of other white horses; the great chalk hill figures of Westbury and Uffington high in my mind. They'd always been icons for me, redolent of our southern chalklands. The great White Horse of Uffington is thought to date from the Bronze Age. Chesterton's Saxons freshly scouring the figure in his Ballad of the White Horse do so not just out of the need for vigilance but as a symbol of the land's vitality after Alfred's victory over the Danes. I always associated the figures as being symbolic of the land itself, ancient monarchs metaphorically uniting with this living symbol of sovereignty; a tradition apparently reflected in the British and Irish taboo against eating horsemeat. I sat with my back to the stone for a while, felt a peace that spoke of a sanctity more immediate than any amount of antiquarians or books.

My path took me up the wooded hill to Kit's Coty House; a lintelled stone formation, once the head of a barrow. I took in the understated but still-sublime views back over the wide valley, past the buildings and now-distant paper mills to the rising hills I'd been in only yesterday. Then I was walking up through the dense, thin yews which creaked a little in the gentle wind. The air felt muggy and overcast now and I stopped at a place at the top of the hill, just off the here-unfrequented path. The yews were interspersed with ash and oak and a fair few semi-fallen trunks. Firepits surrounded by heat-cracked flints

162

announced the presence of former campers as did little bits of fireside paraphernalia; a car wheel hub; blackened and rusty, once used as a hearth; a few old pots and pans and griddles; a stashed, half-eaten packet of KP Skips hinting at a proximate return.

I'd done about ten miles and the campsite I'd had my eye on was still a fair way off. The clear-frequent use of the place made it seem a good spot to stop for the day. After I'd eaten, I put on my new cross, tying the cord carefully by feeling with my fingers. A fox came by a little later, stopped at an adjacent firepit not ten yards away, unaware of my presence and stopping to sniff the air. Lean with a short, summer coat, black hairs among the auburn, it had an air of confidence, experience even, at home on the metaphorical hoof and clearly alive with the height of the season. It stopped there for nearly half a minute, as if it was entirely at ease and then took off with an easy-going gait, down towards the thinner yew trees that ran down the side of the hill, into the descending sun that filtered through the dark branches and needles, seemingly still totally oblivious to me.

That night I felt particularly remorseful. I thought about the things in my life I'd done wrong, both recent and remote, thought about friends I'd like to see upon my return. I wondered whether I could face a return to church going; with fears, unfounded or not, of the hypocrisy of many who attested to the Faith. My burgeoning and recently restored beliefs were clear enough, but political questions still smarted. Any system, any order, perhaps in a natural contrast to its popularity, carries with it criticism, bones of contention and they rallied around in my mind that night. The Christian Church has a long list of discontents and the disgruntled and not without cause. I thought on those issues that rankled the most, already rehearsed. I thought about psychologies of guilt. And the cases of piety taken to extremes; were they a denial of life, of this earth we find ourselves upon, a striving for Heaven while rejecting this very real paradise, or a place that is meant to be so, right here before us? Can striving too hard for ideals make us insufferable, make our world a little colder and more harsh?

None of these thoughts were novel of course. The populism that accompanied Constantine's conversion induced a strange situation which has arguably persisted to this day. The religion, formally associated with suppressed outsiders, had suddenly become respectable. Martyrdom – such a prevalent feature of early Christian life - was no longer a threat. Masses of people flocked in. Faith was suddenly no hardship, sincerity less common, the state not only tolerating the elect but also granting favours.

As for most of us, the Church was something I was brought up with, something I didn't question as a child. And its sense of imbedded institutionalism still puts many off. The Church is seen as part of the establishment, as conventional as a clipped lawn, a monolith from an age redolent with control and over-arching authority, a 'baby' many seem happy to throw out. The Faithful, the thinking seems to go, are living in the past. Many in its number attend out of habit and instruction, do not question the Church or themselves but slide along with an easy complacency. The scandals that have rocked the Catholic Church in particular have been sad milestones in a collective rejection of something people no longer understand or have time for.

But the history of the Christian Church is full of periods of disillusionment spurring renewal, as was the case with many of the orders of monks formed to represent a new beginning, a new ascetic, a renewal of their contract with God. St. Francis's influence is as strong an example of this as any. Praying in a church in San Damiano, not long after his retreat to the cave, he heard Christ on the crucifix say three times: "Francis, go repair my house, which, as you can see, is falling completely to ruins." Francis took this literally and sold off family possessions in order to fund a restoration of the run-down church he was in, to his father's fury. Later, it is thought his auditory vision referred to the wider Church itself.

Adopting a life of simple itinerancy, including a rigour that sometimes saw him throwing himself into icy ditches in winter, he wandered throughout Italy, attracting followers who were soon travelling to France, Germany, Spain, Hungary, Turkey and England preaching repentance, gospel simplicity and obedience to Christ's teaching. The Church was tainted by corruption at that time but due to the Franciscan teaching men and women alike, "rich and worldly, have renounced possessions and, for the love of Christ, turned their backs on the world," as one contemporary put it.

That night I dreamt a bandmate and friends had come to see me, full of good wishes. In a house in Brighton I met up with healers I had once lived with on my return to life in houses. I'd very much fallen on my feet there, back in my home town, my new housemates with twenty years on me, gratifyingly sorted but who still knew how to enjoy themselves. It had been a highly restorative period and I'd many good memories of the time. In my dream there was a sense of reunion and resolution, somehow related to my putting on the cross, a sense of something fundamental but incredibly graceful falling into place.

Brother Christian

Becket made his way to the coast with as much subterfuge as he could muster, hiding in fens and only travelling by night, taking on the alias of 'Brother Christian'. He set sail early on the 2nd November 1164 from Sandwich in Kent, with no baggage, in a skiff, making land four miles away from Gravelines in France, falling exhausted into the shingle. His air of refinement while eating at an inn in Gravelines itself gave him away and he quickly realised he still needed to keep his head down as Henry's cousin Philip of Flanders was keeping an eye out for him. A single admiring look at a passing knight's hawk on the road caused the latter to exclaim; 'either that's the Archbishop of Canterbury or I'm his double!' One of Becket's company simply replied 'Do you really think that the archbishop of Canterbury travels in this style?'

On packhorse, travelling through rain and hail, Becket arrived at the Cistercian Abbey of Clairmarais, blistered, unshaven, stooping and haggard. After hearing of a deputation to the pope for his deposition or suspension, he feared for his safety and fled across the marshes to a hermitage. He stayed hidden there for three days and was given a hero's welcome when he finally arrived at St Bertin's Abbey in Saint-Omer. For the next six years Becket would stay in various French ecclesiastical refuges while power politics played out between him and Henry, King Louis, Pope Alexander and Frederick the Holy Roman Emperor.

Louis, smarting over various fresh machinations of Henry, offered Becket sanctuary but little more, not wanting to provoke all-out war with the English king. Alexander waxed and waned in his support of Becket, fearful of wrong-footing Frederick, still broadly an ally of Henry's and who now supported an antipope. Envoys rattled back and forth between England and Alexander's base, now at Sens, and Becket's various sanctuaries.

Becket made his way to Sens on a charger with attendants from England who had evaded Henry's spies. Cardinals were moved to tears at the story of Becket's ordeal. Becket spread a legal document of the 'ancestral customs' before the court, saying; "See what the king of England has set up against the liberty of the Catholic Church." It proved an effective piece of theatre. Alexander ordered Becket to return the Cistercians, doubtless believing a time under a monastic lifestyle would cool his temper and give him some time to reflect. Perhaps it would make him more inclined to seek reconciliation with the king.

And so Becket took up residence in the Abbey of Pontigny. Though Alexander thought the stay might calm him down, it didn't quite work out like that. Still full of self-recrimination over Clarendon, Becket threw himself into the monks' lifestyle, never one to do anything by halves. He ate only vegetables, kept vigil at night, adopted a very literal hairshirt, regularly scourged himself and would lie in a stream at the break of day, reminiscent of St Francis but making himself ill with abscesses and ulcers. It all induced a state of delirium and he hallucinated he was pleading his case before the pope, only now being assaulted by faeries.

Was this an example of the overarching severity I had felt so circumspect about when on the hill? T.H. White in 'The Once and Future King' portrayed the asceticism of the early Irish monks as redolent of a 'horrible holiness' and the theme has persisted when we think of later monks as 'womanless men, crooked in the cloister of their age' as the bard Robin Williamson has put it. It's clear such self-denial is not for everyone. Nonetheless, asceticism is a tradition to be found in religions and traditions all over the world; a means and route to higher goals. The toil and sometimes challenge of pilgrimage is just one reflection of this, a reflection that some of the greatest rewards come when we earn them or, to put it another way; to gain something you sometimes have to give something up. And perhaps it's not necessarily about self-recrimination or mortification, but about finding a way to set matters right. At any rate we can say that seeking pleasure to the exclusion of all else can often lead to self-destruction. But anything can be overdone, such as those early Christians who, second century texts tell us, sought self-purification by eating only grass, or adopting the lifestyles of beasts.

Friends persuaded Becket to resume a normal diet, cleverly preaching that even penance could be taken to excess. A little equanimity restored, Becket threw himself into his studies, commissioning copies of the Gospels, Old Testament Prophets and the Book of Isiah with borrowed money. He picked up again his study of canon and civil law and acquired copies of Seneca's moral essays including *De Clementia* which involved the correct conduct of rulers and how honest citizens should behave under oppression. With these and other works, including those of St Ambrose and Cicero, he concluded that the responsibility for admonishing over-arching rulers lay with the Church and its ministers.

St Ambrose in particular advised that friendship should always bow to honesty and that none can be true friends to those who attack the Church. It all armed Becket with the arguments he needed to pursue a vendetta with a king he now saw as no better than a biblical tyrant. He resolved to try and govern the Church from the abbey.

On Christmas Day Henry seized Becket's property and that of his clerks, including land and revenue of the Church of Canterbury. The next day he ordered the deportation of the archbishop's relatives, servants and their families and anyone else who had helped him. Some four hundred people were affected; "a most harrowing exodus" according to William fitz Stephen, with babies in cradles and those suckling at the breast among those evicted. The English revenues to the pope were frozen. Doubtless fearing interdict, anyone bringing a letter from the pope into the country was to be hanged or cast adrift in a boat without oars.

Further machinations ensued. At the end of May, Becket left Pontigny after sending a message to Henry's mother that it was no longer time for compromise and that "shortly, very shortly, if we live and God aids us, we shall unsheathe the sword of the Holy Spirit." He travelled 150 miles to Soissons, praying among pilgrims at the shrines of the Virgin Mary, St Gregory and St Drausinus, the latter the patron saint of those about to go into battle or enter a dual. On Whit Sunday, Becket preached at Vezelay where St Bernard had preached the Second Crusade.

Becket spoke as a man possessed, denouncing Henry, looking still gaunt and hollow cheeked, now bearded to boot and looking in all likelihood like some kind of Old Testament prophet. He condemned the Constitutions (Henry's 'customs') of Clarendon and excommunicated all those enforcing or defending them, going on to launch into a series of personal excommunications, only stopping short of including Henry, some thought, due to the king being seriously ill. But he publicly threatened Henry with this if he didn't repent. The pope ratified all this but his position was to be suddenly weakened by Frederick's renewed wish to unseat him. Henry threatened to shift his allegiance to the antipope if Alexander didn't agree to depose Becket, renounce his excommunications and recognise the 'customs'. In an accompanying letter he referred to Thomas as "my betrayer, formerly Archbishop of Canterbury." He subsequently threatened to expel all the Cistercians in England.Henry's position was now in the ascendant. Thomas' eviction from Pontigny was assured and the dispute had widened to include the papal schism. Frederick's army was ready to cross the Alps and it seemed likely Alexander would cave in to the emperor's and Henry's demands. Things seemed as bleak for Becket as at any time since his flight across the Channel.

When Henry tortured one of Becket's couriers, the archbishop began to fear for his life. As Frederick's soldier's advanced, Alexander revoked Becket's power of excommunication again and Becket had to seek (successfully) King Louis' protection with his tenure at Pontigny now over. The pope fled to Benevento. If Henry chose to side with the antipope the Christian world would be riven in two.

At which point malaria and dysentery hit Frederick's army. Several thousands died including a substantial tranche of nobility and the Emperor was forced to retreat. Becket was convinced this was divine intervention and crowed; "Who will dare in the future to obey the will of princes to the Church's shame, by not punishing wrongdoers? Let him dare it who will!" After further negotiations between all sides during which Becket was accused of (and eloquently denied) inciting wars, John of Salisbury warned him that Henry 'seems to want nothing else but your head on a plate.'

Louis, tired of renewed conflict with Henry, sued for a peace agreement. The subsequent meeting would be the first of several over the following two years. In each, the two kings would near reconciliation only to have negotiations scuppered by Becket's arguable intransigence. The first of these took place in early January 1169 at the festival of the Epiphany in a field beneath the frontier town of Montmirail. The two kings pitched pavilions at either end of the field, various followers and their horses and equipment crowding the site, woodsmoke filling the cold, winter air. Frederick sent ambassadors, strengthening Henry's hand who had even suggested, in an effort at engendering goodwill, that he would take the cross for the Holy Land along with Louis. The settlement would deal with the issue of succession of Henry's sons. It was supposed to settle peace between France and England for the next generation. And it would have spelled the end of the exile of Becket's associates.

With so much at stake, Becket was carefully coached. He was told to observe and obey the 'customs', albeit verbally. He wanted to insert another ambiguous, contentious phase; 'saving God's honour' but was talked out of it. But he was still riled with Henry – the issue for him was no longer so much about the 'customs' but the king's assumption that his will was law. He thought that somebody should make a stand or else his legacy would be terrible for future generations.

He was led down from the hilltop town to the field to address the two kings on his knees. All that was needed, Henry reminded him, was his verbal assent to the 'customs'. Becket began his memorised speech. He was willing to observe, he concluded, the customs to win peace and favour and to do all he could in accordance with Henry's will. And then his humility vanished and he actually uttered, as if driven by the will to be a rebel, those few short, fatal and forbidden words; "saving God's honour." Henry erupted. Becket was proud, vain, forgetful of his generosity. Louis simply said to Thomas; "Lord archbishop, do you wish to be

171

more than a saint?"

Peace talks resumed in February in the French Vexin. As far as Henry was concerned, it was the same state of play and he continued to seek observation of the 'customs'. Arbitrators advised him to restore peace and prosperity to Thomas or face the consequences. After Henry's subsequent targeting of Alexander, Louis and Becket, the French king had begun to feel Henry would never honour his promises. At Clairveux on Palm Sunday, Becket issued another round of excommunications. The pope cancelled them, then changed his mind. When he learnt that the excommunications still stood Henry exploded and later said "Do what you like: I don't rate you and your excommunications and doubt if they are worth an egg!"

Becket threatened to place the whole of England under an interdict. Henry declared he was ready to break completely with Rome if it meant defeating Becket. "Cannot I…", he complained, "…who can capture a well-fortified castle every day, capture a single clerk?" He declared that anyone caught with a letter declaring an interdict would be declared a traitor and deported with their entire families. Communications with Becket or the pope were banned. Monks or priests could only leave the country with a special passport. Goods of all Becket's supporters were to be seized.

Another meeting was arranged between the English and French kings, and Becket, just north of Paris at the Abbey of St-Denis in November. Henry offered to forego 'all the evil customs which might enslave the Church' and to return Becket's associates' property. Thomas promised to defer to Henry as his king and "to render unto Caesar what properly belonged to Caesar." But when it came to it Henry stated he had sworn never to give Becket the kiss of peace again. Becket for his part was now convinced the fight had become one between good and evil, never a good perspective for diffusing a situation. Amongst his library were the letters of St Cyprian who stated it was a Christian's duty to resist a heathen ruler, even if it led to martyrdom.

After further mutual reprisals - Henry now planned to have his son crowned by the archbishop of York and closed the ports while Becket placed interdicts on Aquitaine and England itself - yet another peace conference was called at Freteval Castle between Louis and Henry on the 20th July. Becket was to be summoned to receive Henry's peace on the third and final day.

After Henry and Louis had talked, Henry met Becket in a clearing in a forest now known as the Bois des Brulons. The various parties didn't seem to realise it at the time, but the clearing has long gone under the name of 'Traitor's Meadow'. Becket, riled by the issue of the coronation, ranted spectacularly for an hour, reminding Henry he'd once said he'd rather see his son beheaded than crowned by York. He immediately realised he'd gone too far. He rapidly back tracked. Henry, while still appearing genial, responded icily. "I know you will avenge yourself on them," he said, referring perhaps to the bishops who had acted against Becket, "... those who have betrayed you and me until now, by god's providence I shall pay them back according to the deserts of traitors." It wasn't clear just who he meant to punish; Becket's allies or his.

Becket thought he had managed to get out of a difficult moment and, full of relief, dismounted and prostrated himself before Henry. Back at the royal tents Henry declared that their old affection had been fully restored and then withdrew, leaving his subordinates to thrash out a deal. Becket, ascendant in mood but in all likelihood mentally exhausted, became bombastic and condescending - it appeared he was not entirely in control of his own behaviour. He refused to move back into his apartments at court and thereby formally restore the accord until arrangements for his return to England had been properly settled.

Despite prompts, which may have been attempts at manipulation, Becket refused to annul his excommunications. It was possible he couldn't quite believe it all could be so easy, that an actual settlement was finally at hand. Henry himself had to take Thomas aside as an ugly scene developed, telling him not to rise to the courtiers' bait. He then rode back to the nearby castle, declaring the meeting was over.

For Henry it was tactical retreat in the face of interdictions and he had no intention to abandon the customs. He was simply waiting for Becket to slip up, to pursue the vendetta with further attacks. Sure enough, further excommunications ensued.

Three weeks later, Henry contracted malaria, his fever so serious reports came that he had died. When he recovered he made a pilgrimage to Rocamadour where he had prayed before his campaign at Toulouse ten years previously. The next month he was back with his barons, plotting to see how they could thwart the return of Church lands.

Becket meanwhile joined his band of exiles at Sens where he found out his doubts over Henry's sincerity at Freteval where well founded, a writ regarding the return of confiscated property was discovered to include those fateful words: 'saving the honour of my realm'. At the papal court a cardinal proclaimed to Becket's band of semi-outcasts on Henry; "I thought that more had been given to you in appearance than in reality... we know that an Ethiopian cannot easily change his skin nor a leopard change his spots." Had Becket been right all along?

Memorials

I woke just after four with the very first light. Up at the top of a hill, past a waymarking stone that said thirty-four miles to Canterbury, the track led out to a field over some kind of triple-stoned sarsen stile. The sun - just emerging from a plantation over a field of dew-laden crops, bluish green - was clear and cool though piercingly bright.

The way took me along the ridge by the sloping tree line to my right, fields studded with pylons stretching out on the flat high ground to my left. After a couple of miles, the path dropped down a lane to cross an A-road via an ungainly bridge. There was a memorial to a girl who'd died on the road here which may or may not have been instrumental in the constructional of the high, metal bridge, a grim reminder of DfT machinations where only a certain number of fatalities necessitate provision of safe crossings. As if thrown by all this, I somehow lost my way temporarily on the far side as a minor footpath turned tangential and counterintuitive down the following slope.

But I recovered myself and was soon heading through the small village of Detling, opting to stick to the tarmacked road on the low ground, the ridge rising up to my left. I didn't fancy an unnecessary climb and I was aware of the need to score some water sooner rather than later. In any case this was likely the historic way and was even signposted The Pilgrims' Way for cyclists.

At a crossroads not that far down the road I found the timber frames of The Cock Horse, replete with swing-board sign whose image was comprised of a monk leading a medieval lady on a horse with a scallop shell backdrop. It was all quiet but would surely be open soon I thought and I went to sit down on a bench under a window. A woman rapped at the glass as I did so and opened the casing. They'd be open in an hour she told me, hoover in hand, and I weighed up waiting for that long, the prospect of a coffee high on my mind. The fact that it was still only seven in the morning and I'd been walking for a while leant events a strange feeling. In the end though an hour seemed too long to while away on a roadside bench, even where coffee was concerned and I upped and got on my way along the already-dusty road.

I took a turning to find a church and – I hoped - water but both proved elusive and I found myself on a bridleway parallel to the Pilgrims' Way, which became a footpath through grass to the side of a wheatfield, magpies suggesting I'd done something wrong. The second church I'd tried, down a track into a village, appeared no better at first. When I finally found it, two men were standing in a separate enclave of the churchyard by a memorial cross with its poppies. A third man with them was in a wheelchair, too young to rightfully be so, and I wondered what foreign field he may have found himself in and what exactly had happened to him there. They had a palpable air about them of grief and bitterness.

I thought of the sickening waste of young men and women sent out to fight for confused priorities so far away where poppies held such a different currency. I thought about mercy, or lack of it, the calculus of 'blood and treasure', justifications and calls to withdraw scrabbling for advantage while we all bore witness to the loss. Whatever the rights and wrongs of our presence in Afghanistan, our soldiers fought for an ideal, for the hope of leaving a better country behind. But so many paid the ultimate sacrifice or had their lives irrevocably marred. How much of the welfare of these wounded soldiers and their families, I wondered, were now discarded along with yesterday's news, jettisoned with the very memory of conflict? Can we not at least properly honour and compensate them for what they had had to endure?

I found a tap eventually, just above green water in a square lead tank. I sat in the wooden-roofed porch to the churchyard for a while, studying my map and seeing to my blisters. Two women, middle aged, came through to clean the church or change the flowers, studiously ignoring me but glancing at my map; curious, wary at once. For my part I was just glad to be in the shade as the sun continued to rise and very grateful for the water.

The day was a combination of covering miles and trudging along the lane without much of a view for the most part. But here and there you could see the landscape gently rolling south; woods and fields and pasture folding over one another like some kind of subtle dream. Presently I passed my first Kentish orchard, oast houses eventually presenting themselves; two together in twin peaks, another one converted with windows revealing three floors. Yet another with a weather vane shaped as a centaur. Two of them rectangular, their roofs topped with fluted, white hats.

Oast houses, designed to dry hops, can be found in other counties too. But we most often associate them with Kent and seeing them here was another reminder of how far I'd come. Hops tend to be dried industrially these days, the oast houses (or just 'oasts') given over to luxury housing: domesticated, rural curios. It was perhaps another sign of the hidden infrastructure of that which governs our lives today, the surviving heritage appendaged as a nod to former days when beauty and craftmanship were more closely grafted to the everyday mechanics of our lives.

I found a track towards a picnic spot that took me uphill, past a post with a carved kestrel, another post shaped in the image of knapweed, gigantic. I sat beneath a beech in the shade, taking in the blueish view and was glad to get off the interminable track. Belloc talks approvingly of the road here, that it could be "taken as a type of what the primitive wayfarers intended when the conditions offered them for their journey were such as they would have chosen out of all." There was a sense of easy conviviality with the path. There were no undulations, no great feats of labour required. Canterbury grew a little closer by a pace. All that was needed was to keep heading on. The combination of the long miles for the day, the unbroken heat, the unrelenting flatness and unerring nature of the track leant proceedings a kind of hypnotism. It gave you time to think, or go beyond your thoughts with the momentum of already-covered miles.

"It is peculiar in England," Belloc goes on, "...this county of Kent, and especially its valleys. I had known it hitherto only as a child, a stranger, but no one who has visited it in childhood can forget the sheep in the narrow lanes, or the leaning cones of the hop-kilns against the sky : the ploughlands under the orchards : all the Kentish Weald."

I saw no sheep but a man pushed a dog in a pram; a Chinese-looking pug-nosed breed and such was the state of mild hallucination it seemed the most natural thing in the world. At Hollingbourne, I passed 'The Dirty Habit'; an old-looking brown-bricked pub, closed for the morning, inferring silent slight. It's a familiar trope, that may owe much to Chaucer's cast of characters in The Canterbury Tales. Though his pilgrims took the route of Watling Street from London, via Rochester - a route I would not meet with till later on - his account is of course perhaps the primary source people turn to when we think of medieval English pilgrimage in general and the Pilgrims' Way in particular. And among the 'verray parfit gentil Knight', the Franklin, the coarse and entertaining Miller and the extensive marital political musings of the Wife of Bath we have the Monk with his tales of downfall of the illustrious, often through pride; the devious, extorting Pardoner and in particular the mutually hostile Friar and Summoner, carving rhetorical chunks off each other.

Friars formed part of the 'regular' clergy who adhered to the jurisdiction of their order and were answerable to the pope. As such, they were distinguished from both older monastic orders' allegiance to a particular monastery and 'secular' clergy such as parish priests under the sway of their bishop. The Dominican and Franciscan friars; beggars and preachers, redolent with innovation, were an example of the reformative power of the papacy. We tend to think of the pope as an almost almighty, if not archaic, source of traditional authority, contentiously so or otherwise but the office was once far less reactionary than the more localised system of archbishops and bishops under its sway. Papal support of St Francis's reforms was one example of this. But the parish priests whose place was threatened by the friars - with the latter's powers to preach, hear confession and give absolution - did not always take kindly to these incomers. These regular clergy came to be treated with suspicion, loyal as they were to a foreign power, like reds under the bed; not least in Chaucer's day, when the Hundred Years' War was in full flight and the papacy resided in Avignon.

Friars in particular were widely seen as of questionable morals; fornicating, peddling relics and the indulgences which would do so much to discredit the medieval church. The Summoner and Pardoner of Chaucer's Tales were later innovations of the papacy and another breed again. Recruited to make money for the Church, they often lacked much real piety themselves and were apparently prone to ranting and fanaticism. Summoners were ecclesiastical officials, employed by bishops' courts to summon sinners to trial. Pardoners, a kind of friar themselves, held papal license to sell pardons and indulgences and were not necessarily in holy orders. Those they inspired to imitate them were even worse. If Chaucer wrote in a time when the lustre of the friars had grown dim, his treatment of the Pardoner shouts loud about the resentment of these particular preachers many must have felt.

As far as the friars and monks go - the former travelling mendicants, to be distinguished from the cloistered monks of the abbeys - perhaps our view of them has been coloured by apologists for the Reformation. We can sometimes think of the monks as lazy and covetous whereas the friars were out for a good time, boozing and womanising. Even in his day Chaucer was not immune to such views. In the *'Tales*, he poked fun at people of all ranks and the clergy were certainly not immune. But the Friar and Pardoner come in for special treatment. There is a story in fact that Chaucer in his youth was fined for fighting with a friar in Fleet Street which would help account for any later animosity.

Such are the crimes of the Summoner in the Friar's Tale that he is eventually carted off to Hell. The Summoner for his part describes the special place for friars in that domain and has the friar in his tale as a lecher and insincere extortionist who begs in return for supposedly making prayers for the dead but who, payment received, wipes his ledger clean on leaving each house. His fate is perhaps not so bad as that described in the Friar's Tale, suffice to say he gets wind of his come-uppance in spectacular fashion.

Chaucer comes closer to revealing his full views on the heart of the matter when his Host addresses The Monk;

'God send confusion on the foolish skunk

That first persuaded you to be a monk!

180

You would have put a hen to pretty use,

Had you permission as you have the juice

To exercise your pleasure in procreation!

You could have done your part to build the nation.

Alas, who put you in so wide a cope?

Damnation take me but if I were Pope,

Not only you but many a mighty man

Going about the world with tonsured pan

Should have a wife; for look, the world's forlorn!

Religion has got hold of all the corn...'

It is highly likely that Chaucer, as a sympathiser with John Wyclif, was in favour of a married clergy. Wyclif was a headstrong, hot-headed reformer who challenged the supremacy of the pope. He also tackled issues around property and wealth and argued the ecclesiastical estate should hold no possessions besides those needed for the very basics of survival. As such his supporters included John of Gaunt, third son of Edward III and one of the richest and most influential men of the day. Gaunt was keen for a rationale to plunder the Church to raise money for the French wars and to stop sending cash to the Avignon-based papacy.

Wyclif's followers became known as the Lollards, which might have come from the Flemish for 'idler'. He had supporters at Court and in the Commons who came to be known as the 'Lollard Knights'; a mixture of avaricious plunderers and genuine reformers, many of them friends of Chaucer's. Wyclif was also critical of pilgrimage and it has even been suggested that the '*Tales* are a parody of pilgrimage. In any case, Wyclif's favour fell, though his followers' did not and he was ascribed as being one of the expounders of the sense of 'The New Movement' of the time which eventually led to the Peasant's Revolt; a movement John of Gaunt and the Lollard Knights had broadly supported till the rioting itself. Even Richard II, for all his later faults, had agreed to the rebels' demands and offered to be their leader till he was later overruled by the barons, a sign that, as G. K. Chesterton has pointed out, the monarchy in the Middle Ages could be far more progressive than even in Tudor times with that age's obsession with the cult of the Prince.

Wyclif, with his writings going on to question the value of Mass and the sacrament itself had overstepped the mark before all this. Had things gone another way, his 'simple preachers', rebelling against the friars much as the friars themselves had once rebelled against the monks might have been absorbed into an evolving church. But his influence was clear and is relevant today with his thoughts on a celibate clergy, something that only became formally mandatory in the Eleventh Century, although this may have followed a much older tradition stemming back to at least the Fourth Century. Some think the Eleventh Century edict was introduced chiefly as a means to secure ecclesiastical lands as the property of the Church, rather than risk them being divided among inheritors.

Still, Chaucer was a moderate. His finest religious sentiments in the '*Tales* often come from the representatives, like the Parson, of religious institutions that Wyclif disapproved of. Chaucer mocked the Friar and the rest but didn't hate them. They took their place among the diverse panoply making their way to Canterbury; the devout, the refined and the crude.

Strings of spring-line villages decked the way, albeit a little off the path. Harrietsham, Hollingbourne, Lenham. The Pilgrims' Way may have once been their means of connection and the plain here is drained by the Len, a stream that runs eventually to the Medway. As Belloc points out, by Lenham there is an almost invisible watershed;

"a parting of no moment, not a ridge, hardly observable to one standing above it on the hillside... the dividing line between the basins of the Medway and the Stour. All the hydrology of south-eastern England presents this peculiarity. The watersheds are low; the low ranges do not divide the river basins, because the water system is geologically older than the Chalk Hills."

As I crossed a minor road, a sign warned of the presence of poisonous caterpillars. I didn't think much of it till suddenly a dozen or so, hanging from a tree, lurid in yellow and black and wriggling venomously, were now dangling from the brim of my hat like tiny abseiling assassins. At which very moment half a dozen spandex-clad cyclists appeared behind me and I had to almost jump out of the way, entailing a great effort not to come into contact with the hairy grubs at the same time. Immediately behind the cyclists were four or five off-road motorbikers, necessitating further escapist manoeuvres on my part. It was about the most hectic thing that had happened all day. Suddenly the track was very quiet again.

I passed a war memorial cut into the chalk of the hill in the shape of a cross to my left. Chaucer himself had fought and been taken a prisoner in France, some thirty years prior to his writing of the *'Tales'*. His feelings on his experiences can be glimpsed in The Knight's Tale with its description of a temple dedicated to Mars, a portrayal of the terror of

183

warfare up there with Brueghel or Goya. But 'Troilus and Criseyde', his great epic based on the classical story, shows the regard in which he held the chivalric principles of courage and honour. His friends in the 'Lollard Knights' were heavily present in the crusades. Wyclif himself had announced that "wars waged for God's justice, or for the honour of Christ are right and no other." A pity then that the crusades were often choosing enemies for the simple fact they were not Christian, such as the Baltic pagans.

The grievance that led to The Hundred Years War that Chaucer had fought in stemmed back to Henry II when he married Eleanor and so inherited Aquitaine. It was Edward III's refusal to continue to offer the French king homage that helped lead to the conflict, his adopting the Fleur de Lis as well as the three leopards as symbols of the joint English and, in aspiration, French kingship. The origins of the war are complex and were certainly partly provoked by France's antagonism by supporting Scotland, England's foes of the day. But there can be no doubt of Edward III's grandstanding, just as, whatever the original causes, for the greater swathe of the conflict the English were very much the aggressors. The war was also a product of the overly militarised states of Europe. Tournaments, martial prowess were enshrined as the classical pastimes and values. When devoting energy into the distant crusades became no longer tenable, France and England fell into fighting one another as if it were somehow an honourable pursuit, as if it were the most natural thing in the world; an overtly romanced bookend to a belligerent age.

Lenham Hillside Cross is dedicated to the fallen of the two world wars; the first never so needless, cruel and futile, the second never so grimly necessary. They were both meant to be the war to end all wars. Chesterton's Ballad of the White Horse had in some ways anticipated the conflagrations of the Twentieth Century with its critique of the likely trajectory of a cult of violence and the nihilism and idea of the 'overman' as espoused by figures like Nietzsche. As the poet and preacher Malcolm Guite has written, Chesterton wrote of a courage brooked not by the chance of victory but 'a joy without cause.' The vigilance espoused in the last book of the ballad; 'The Scouring of the Horse', is one of the maintenance of old truths by constant renewal and the resistance of tyranny wherever it is found.

As I sat in the shade of bushes on a nearby tangential footpath an older walker in white shorts and t-shirt came by, a veteran of better and worse days perhaps, complaining slightly of the lack of view and unvarying nature of the track. Kites and buzzards curled in the air above us. Another time my journey would be accompanied by a spitfire overhead, rolling and rolling in the summer sun above the green and golden fields just as they once had done some seventy-five years ago, preserving our freedom at such a high cost. Time folded in on itself; there would always be spitfires it seemed, we would always remember that fight, that sacrifice, we would always be singing the song of this garden of England.

Such imagery has been hijacked at times by those who'd turn our heritage into a caricature of a golden age of boozers and village greens in a pretext for sabotaging the project for a unified continent that Churchill himself had helped bring about. Have we been at all complacent in our national dream, our notion of ourselves buoyed by ancient victory? The story of the last war is always more complex than that; our victory came at a terrible price, not least the bombardments of the German hinterlands that were arguably as much punitive as expedient, a sign perhaps of warfare to come when the terrible tally of aerial bombardment should

185

be as much of a deterrent for any war as it is possible to have.

We cannot give in to fantasies every bit as short of the grinding realities as those of romanticised notions of medieval knights who stood for so much when Middle Age warfare was full of a bitter attrition. All the same the servicemen who did not want to fight but signed up nonetheless speak of a bravery that shouldn't have to be repeated. If we truly can work towards peace that selflessness can express something of how the world is meant to be; a place of synthesis and harmony, promised for so long and hopefully still within our grasp. Chesterton's prescription for what would prove the fall from grace of the strife of the two world wars was to cultivate humility and joy.

I slept in a campsite that night, bowed to the immediacy of an actual tap in the field by the path, had a shower. A young couple pulled up in an old-style red and green camper van and they later asked me to join them, plied me with food, intuitive and likeable, a Kiwi and her partner, embarking on careers. It was enough to restore my faith in humanity. I was sorry to miss them the following morning when I rose and departed before they were up, shaking my tent after a light shower of rain. There was now just one more day to Canterbury, the prospect of it immanent, surreal.

Martyrdom

When Henry met Becket at Tours in October 1170 to prepare for the latter's return to England he treated his archbishop with total disdain, subsequently moving his entire court fifteen miles upstream without telling Thomas. At a later meeting, things went better and they talked for some time, as though their friendship had been properly restored. But Henry asked of him, "Oh, why is it that you won't do what I want? Because for certain, if you would, I'd put everything into your hands." Becket saw this as akin to Satan's temptation of Christ. As they left, having made arrangements for Becket's return, he turned to Henry and said; "My lord, something tells me that I now take leave of you and that in this life you will see me no more."

Henry ordered for all lands and livings to be restored that had been taken from the exiles. There were reports that bailiffs were asset stripping Canterbury lands – representatives of the exiles were reinstated and summarily evicted again. Becket had made particular foes of three bishops; Roger of Pont l'Eveque, Gilbert Foliot and Jocelin of Salisbury. Roger was a longstanding rival of Becket's and subsequent archbishop of York. Foliot had been a probable aspirant for the archiepiscopric and was an enemy of Becket from the start. Becket had had him excommunicated at Clairvaux along with Jocelin. Dubbed 'the delinquent bishops' they all schemed to hinder him now, doubtless fearing more reprisals from his direction.

But Becket was regarded as a hero in Canterbury, not least thanks to the behaviour of the de Brocs, Henry's old whoremasters and general hired thugs, who were busy looting, hoarding, vandalising property and killing stock.

On hearing of Becket's return they had scoured the Channel and when they had found one of his transport vessels they took the wine and murdered or incarcerated the crew.

Nonetheless, Becket still sought rapprochement and wrote to the pope saying he wanted Henry to be treated as charitably as possible. In writing to Henry he voiced his fears of imprisonment or worse, stating than Ranulf de Broc had been overhead boasting of murdering him "before he can eat a whole loaf in England". Thomas went on; "Fate is drawing me, unhappy wretch that I am, to that afflicted Church; by your license and grace I shall return to her, perhaps to die to prevent her destruction...".

It seemed clear that Henry wanted Thomas' full submission and acceptance of the 'customs'. Nonetheless Becket praised him for his acts of kindness towards him and the exiles and hoped Henry would honour his promises if he was treated patiently. At which point Alexander ordered the excommunication of the three delinquent bishops and decreed that Becket be made papal representative for England once again.

This ought to have spelt victory for Becket but he was facing a stronger temptation than Henry's wish for acquiescence; his old impulsiveness if not his actual pride. When Henry didn't meet him at Rouen as planned, Becket became argumentative towards his hosts. He was subsequently warned that the de Brocs and three bishops were scouring the coast for boats with decrees and meant to have his head. Becket managed to deliver the excommunications to the bishops via a boy who staunchly traced them to a church in Dover and, having delivered the writs, ran off and hid, quite sensibly, in a nearby market.

Becket made a swift and uneventful crossing on the 1st of December. But de Broc and a band of weapon-wielding men were waiting for him at Sandwich. They ransacked the baggage and made threats before John of Salisbury somehow managed to curb their behaviour. Becket and his entourage then took the road for Canterbury, twelve miles away.

Bells pealed, people sang, parishioners processed with crosses as he passed. Crowds turned out, threw clothes in the road, begged for blessings. Becket was hailed as 'the father of the orphans and the judge of the widows'. Archbishops were used to lavish welcomes but this was something altogether more spectacular. It certainly outweighed any entry Henry had ever made. In Canterbury people wore their Sunday best. Organs, trumpets, choristers sounded in the cathedral and the whole city was decked as if it was a festival. Comparisons were even made to Christ's entry into Jerusalem. When Becket preached to the gathered monks in the chapter-house he took for his text 'Here we have no abiding city, but we seek one to come.'

Henry's officers appeared the following day, demanding the sentences on the three bishops be lifted. Becket refused and the bishops sailed for Normandy, accusing Becket of seeking to depose Prince Henry and raising an army to fight him. It was a false accusation, spuriously based on that older bone of contention; Becket's insistence that he alone had the right to crown the young prince and not the Archbishop of York, an insistence that had hampered the delivery of the coronation. When Becket travelled to London to try and make amends with the young Henry he was refused entry and told to return to Canterbury. There was still a huge reception amongst the common people for Becket in London and he for his part was mystified that the young prince could behave like this. But he was warned that he and Salisbury were in danger of assassination. On hearing this he touched his neck; "Here, here is where the knaves shall get me."

Canterbury was under a state of siege when he returned on 18th December with de Broc's men placed at gateways

189

and other key sites. They brutalised the inhabitants with death threats, took provisions from those who supplied the archbishop, poached his deer, stole his dogs, beat his servants and cut off the tail of one of his packhorses.

On Christmas Day Becket preached that he had returned to lift the yoke of servitude or to suffer death among his people. He then excommunicated those occupying the Canterbury lands, singling Robert de Broc out for particular opprobrium. After high mass the next day he sent messengers to King Louis stating the agreement made at Freteval was at an end. They wept as he dismissed them with a final blessing, believing he only wanted them out of the way so they could be spared his increasingly likely-seeming fate. He gave a note to be delivered to one of his loyal bishops; 'Farewell for ever' it read.

The 'delinquents' met Henry in Barfleur where they perpetuated their slander of Becket challenging Prince Henry's coronation and positioning himself at the head of a small army. Henry banged his fists together on hearing this. "It is not for us to say what should be done," they said, adding; "…while Thomas lives you will have neither peace nor quiet, nor see good days."

Subsequently, Henry tried Becket for life and liberty without even sending him a summons. The barons and ecclesiastical worthies who had presided at Northampton six years previously gathered again. The charge was raised to one of treason, Henry declaring Becket had effectively declared war on him by trying to deny Prince Henry his crown. After Henry went on to label Becket as evil and dangerous, further charges were sent to the pope, the bishop Arnulf of Lisieux stating Thomas had damaged the Church by not moderating his zeal to suit the times and by not giving enough time for the excommunicated to repent.

The barons encouraged a death sentence. Henry decreed that Becket should be captured. It was here, or hereabouts - a few days earlier than the court hearing perhaps - that Henry was meant to have uttered those instrumental words; "Who will rid me of this turbulent priest?". That phrase however comes from an Eighteenth Century 'New History of England'. Contemporary reports are a little more colourful and show all the clearer Henry's frustration at subordinates paying deference to the Church, together with grievance at Becket's ingratitude and presumption. There are various versions but that of Edward Grim goes like this:

"What miserable drones and traitors have I nourished and promoted in my realm, who let their lord be treated with such shameful contempt by a low-born clerk!" Another source goes on: *"A man who has eaten my bread, who came to my court poor and I have raised him high – now he draws up his heel to kick me in the teeth! He has shamed my kin, shamed my realm: the grief goes to my heart, and no one has avenged me!"* Gervase of Canterbury has the final words: *"How many cowardly, useless drones have I nourished that not even a single one is willing to avenge me of the wrongs I have suffered!"*

It was typical Henry, albeit taken to decisive heights. It was to become all too clear that not everyone around him knew his moods and knew that they often blew over. The four knights who acted on his words were unimportant but ambitious with it too and saw a chance to raise their favour. The fact that they had been threatened with forfeiture of property, as they or their fathers had been Stephen's men in the civil war (a redistribution that may have been presided over by Becket), could only have further spurred them to act.

191

And so Reginald fitz Urse, William de Tracey, Richard Brito and Hugh de Morville set sail for England. They rested at Saltwood Castle where they gathered a small force with the aid of the de Brocs. Stealthily, they made their way through Canterbury and into the courtyard of the Archbishop's Palace while others ordered citizens to take up arms in the name of the king and head to the palace as well. The citizens refused to do so and the knights' men ordered a curfew, instructing all to "stay indoors and keep the peace, no matter what they might see or hear". The best troops were ordered to position themselves to stop any rescue attempt and prevent any chance of escape. Becket had foreseen this noose of course and perhaps one of the greatest questions that remain is whether he submitted to it willingly or even willed it on. Perhaps he saw it as the inevitable result of a trajectory that had been playing out for years. Was this what it meant to be more than a saint?

+   +   +

The four knights, with drink taken, entered the archbishop's court, leaving their chainmail and weapons beneath a mulberry tree before storming into the great hall where the monks were finishing their dinner. The clergymen began to melt away after Thomas appeared but the archbishop bade them stay guessing only too accurately what might occur if he was left alone with these men of the king.

The knights found themselves at a loss for words besides the overbearing fitz Urse and a lively interchange ensued between him and Becket. Fitz Urse accused him of wanting to unseat Prince Henry, stating that the king had ordered Becket leave the kingdom.

"Stop threatening me Reginald," said Thomas. *"I put my trust in the king of heaven and from this day forward refuse to leave my church. Once I fled like a timid priest. Now I have returned to my church in the counsel and obedience of the lord pope. I have not come back to flee again: anyone who wants can find me here."*

When fitz Urse questioned whose authority he served, that of the pope or the king, asking flatly whether he recognised he owed everything to the king, Thomas replied "we must render to Caesar the things that are Caesar's and to God the things that are God's." Fitz Urse continued to grind away, decrying the Christmas excommunications and saying Thomas ought to show obedience to the king.

"If all the swords of England," Thomas retorted, *"...were aimed at my head, your threats could not dislodge me from my observance of God's justice and my obedience to the lord pope. I tell you I shall strike at anyone who violates the right of the pope or Christ's Church. I will not spare him, nor will I delay to impose ecclesiastical sentences upon him."*

When this provoked threats he went on; *"Are you then come to slay me? If so I shall commit myself and my cause to the great judge of mankind. I am not moved by threats, nor are your swords more ready to strike than is my soul for martyrdom. Find someone else to frighten – you will find me steadfast in the battle of the Lord."*

The knights commanded the remaining monks to seize Becket in the king's name before storming out, bundling two servants of the archbishop along with them. De Broc's men piled into the courtyard. Bolting the gate behind them, the knights gathered their swords and armour.

Inside, as Becket sought to reassure his clerks, John of Salisbury attempted to calm the archbishop himself down, questioning if he had inflamed things further in his treatment of the knights. Becket, while typically impulsive, may still have had a better handle on the reality of the situation. "May God's will be done," was his final response.

The knights and other men tried to force entry to the hall before trying a back route led on by Robert de Broc who had occupied the palace in Becket's long absence and so knew the place well. As they smashed their way in through shuttered windows, the gathered monks begged Becket to take refuge in the cathedral. The bell for vespers called a calm Thomas on. Somehow unbolting a jammed door, monks manhandled Becket into the heart of the cathedral, shutting it immediately behind him.

As the monks at vespers rushed to meet him, Becket, having protested that "the Church is a house of prayer and is not to be made into a fortress," walked up the steps to the high altar. Fitz Urse barged in. "Where is Thomas Becket," he cried, "…traitor to the king and the kingdom?" "Here I am," Thomas replied. "What do you want from me? I am no traitor to the king but a priest." He could easily have hidden but chose to face the men. Refusing the shouted order to absolve the excommunicated and told he was about to be put to death he said; "I am ready to die for my Lord, so that in my blood the Church may obtain peace and liberty," forbidding any harm be visited on his men.

As the knights bore down on him all but three of his followers ran to hide. The knights attempted to wrestle Thomas outside but he clung to a pillar. As the struggle escalated Thomas cried; "I will not leave this church. If you wish to kill me you must kill me here." Anticipating blows he covered his head and prayed aloud.

William de Tracey struck first, slicing through the top of Becket's cranium and into his shoulder with his sword. Edward Grim, Thomas's man, threw his arms round the archbishop, one of which was almost removed in the process. With blood pouring down his face Thomas continued praying. De Tracey struck at his head again and Thomas fell, uttering as he lay prone; "For the name of Jesus and the protection of the Church I am ready to embrace death." Brito smote off the top of his head, sparks flying in the dim light as his sword shattered on the stones below. A retrobate clerk in attendance to de Mourville, stamped on Becket's neck, scooping out his brains with his sword and smearing them over the pavings, shouting "this one won't rise again." The knights then ransacked Becket's gold and plate and money in his coffers before riding for Saltwood, leaving the de Brocs to comprehensively strip the palace.

The monks left Becket's body alone for hours but - after the de Brocs had finished looting - a crowd came into the cathedral, gathering around the archbishop's form. Some cut or tore off clothing to dip in his blood, others daubed their eyes with it, hoping for a cure to poor sight, yet more attempted to fill little phials. When the monks cleared away the onlookers, Becket's brains were dutifully scooped up and placed in a silver basin. His skull was bound in a white cloth and body placed before the high altar. He was hastily buried the next day in the crypt after the de Brocs threatened to desecrate the body.

Insurgence

Henry shut himself in his chamber for three days then entered penitential seclusion for a further forty. The pope was so shocked, he refused to see an Englishman for three weeks. Eleanor, quite likely disgusted with the whole affair, left England for Aquitaine. A papal interdict was placed on Henry's French lands. Suddenly an international pariah, he opted to lie low by dealing with affairs in Ireland, setting sail towards the end of the following year.

He returned seven months later and made public penance at Avranches Cathedral. He promised to provide 200 knights to the Knights Templar, to take the cross or fight in Spain, to return the confiscated Canterbury lands and abolish those 'customs' detrimental to the Church. For a time, it seemed some sense of former order was restored. But, as many in the European nobility were still aggrieved, none of these things were enough. The following year, 1173, Henry's entire family - Eleanor and his three sons - rose against him. From utter ascendency Henry was suddenly laid low, its highly personal nature making the rebellion an only too bitter reversal of fortune. Many thought that Becket's end had 'brought the wrath of heaven' upon Henry. Chroniclers said of the war; 'the Lord's martyr... seemed to seek vengeance for the innocent blood.' 'The kingdoms of the earth' they said 'were overthrown, churches laid waste, religion dragged through the mire and peace lost throughout the land.'

Henry's marriage with Eleanor had been a partnership for power from the start, for them both, more than just brought about by affection. She had never been shy and retiring and had accompanied Louis on crusade in 1146 where, legend has it, she led a contingent of bare-breasted women warriors. But she was disaffected with Louis, claiming she had married someone 'more monk than a man' and quickly realised that Henry, when he appeared, eighteen years old and fresh from fighting Stephen in 1151, could provide for her the power she desired. She is thought to have been twenty-nine. For Henry, she offered him riches and land. Within months of the meeting, Eleanor had divorced Louis. The new couple certainly didn't exactly hang about and they were famously said to have 'shattered the Ten Commandments on the spot' upon meeting. They married in secret in 1152. Louis would never forgive the slight.

For such a famous figure, surprisingly little is known about Eleanor. On her brother's death, she became the heir to Aquitaine. When her father died suddenly on pilgrimage to Santiago, two days away from the city, she was suddenly made duchess. The dukes and duchesses of Aquitaine (the latter rarer even in the more liberal south) had traditionally only paid nominal allegiance to the Frankish kings further north, which is why her lands had been such a prize for the two kings. Her various legends precede her - she has been painted as sex-obsessed and power-driven and conversely well-learned and a paradigm of virtue, a lover of the arts and power house behind the troubadours and their courts of courtly love; she was styled by some as their very queen. She has been an inspiration for writers for the best part of a millennium but nearly all of these writings are fiction; the truth is the historians know very little about her, perhaps partly due to Henry later writing her out of the records in spite. She was certainly demonised by chroniclers for centuries. But her children regarded her fondly and it is thought their father's treatment of her was a large part of the cause of the rebellion.

Maintaining control over Aquitaine was her primary goal, whether or not Henry realised as much. As the years rolled by after the murder of Becket her trust in her husband steadily corroded. By the time of the rebellion she had probably decided he had given her all the authority he was ever likely to – ultimate power would always be his, if unchallenged. As far as she was concerned, she ought to have been on an equal footing with Henry; Aquitaine was hers and she didn't want it subsumed into the Angevin empire upon his death. When Henry granted Gascony – one fifth of Aquitaine - as part of their daughter's dowry she was furious. He didn't help matters by further ignoring her and accepting a rival's homage for Toulouse, disregarding her claims to the territory.

By all accounts a loving father he had, he thought, been at pains to keep his offspring happy. Geoffrey was to inherit Brittany; Richard, Aquitaine; for young Henry, Normandy, Maine, Anjou and of course England itself. John, poor John, seems not to have been in line for much and the moniker 'Lackland' stems from this time, despite his later loss of such vast territories when made king. But however fond Henry may apparently have been towards his sons, he was an absent father. And his sons in all probability bore grudges against him for his heavy-handed style. Henry himself had been groomed for leadership from an early age while they were simply living in his shadow. Henry the Young in particular was frustrated at having been crowned and yet not granted any particular powers.

Henry ruled his family autocratically, including choosing his sons' brides and household employees. He masked this iron will with seeming warmth, but his feelings gave way to the familiar explosiveness, a controlling streak determining his outbursts, be they angry or tearful or joyous. Perhaps he thought his sons were not ready to rule. Perhaps he never gave them a chance to prove otherwise.

Louis had seen in all this a chance to sow the seeds of discord and it was under his influence the revolt came about.

While the rebellion of his three sons must have been painful, the main threat to Henry came from the French king. In addition, many English nobles thought Henry owed them money or land or both. He was blamed for being overbearing in his manners and for 'trampling upon the necks of the proud and haughty'. As with the state of the law, Henry had sought restoration of his grandfather's property as well which could only have put noses out of joint. He wished to be seen as gracious in his rule but only if such overtures did nothing to diminish his out and out supremacy in any given situation. In particular, his refusal to grant concessions to Eleanor or their children would ultimately cost him their very allegiance.

When, on turning eighteen in February 1173, Henry the Young insisted he be granted control over at least some of his lands, his father rebuffed him. The young king-in-waiting bolted for Louis' - now his father-in-law's - court, departing in the middle of the night. The French king wound him round his finger. Stoked by Eleanor's mounting grievances, the other boys defected as well. As Henry's soldiers flooded into Aquitaine, Eleanor made to join her sons but was captured by Henry en route.

'The Great Revolt' lasted for over a year and entailed a war on six fronts with 40 sieges, skirmishes or battles. By June the rebellion had spread far and wide throughout Henry's empire. He would need every iota of his powers to meet it. He was victorious of course; he had superior tactics and judgement and he inspired great loyalty in his men. But the revolt was still an incredible psychological blow. When he temporarily succeeded in defeating it, wiping out a Breton force at Dol, he could have humiliated his sons but instead offered them castles and cash. But money was not what they craved. At a peace conference in September in Gisors, Louis continued to stir things up and when a certain Robert of Leicester screamed at Henry and made to attack him, the

English king walked out in disgust.

Robert then invaded England and though the rebel force was again subsequently defeated, Louis and Henry's sons fought on against their stubborn but horrified father. But even after the defeat of the rebels in Brittany, Louis, Philip of Flanders and Henry the Young continued to fight. Eleanor was interred in Salisbury Castle. She would remain imprisoned for most of the rest of her husband's life. Henry later said the war was akin to an eagle being attacked and overcome by its very own chicks. He actually had a mural commissioned of just such a scene in his chambers at Winchester and would subsequently meditate upon it, determined to never forget.

Henry was in many ways an archetype of strong medieval kingship. His lands, so extensive, made him 'the most powerful man north of the Alps' and 'the most famous man in Christendom' as some had it. No one since Charlemagne had held so much European land and his reign was harked back to by subsequent English kings as a golden age and pretext for their territorial aggression. But he was also a model of overarching control. The incident with Becket and the beggar and the cloak revealed his knack of humiliating subordinates at court but speaks volumes too about the way he would wield power over foes farther flung.

He styled himself 'Henry, by the grace of god, king of the English, duke of the Normans, duke of the Aquitarians and count of the Angevins.' He desired most of all to be seen as a solid and astute monarch. Often gracious when triumphant, if defeated he was not above horrific demonstrations of power such as torching the land at Toulouse or his reprisals towards Welsh rebels. In total control of his lands, he was constantly on the move, and often slept little. He was 'at the centre of a tornado' and he wouldn't have wanted it any other way. Is it any wonder if he doubted his sons could fill his shoes?

No Man's Orchard

I walked near a ridge full of trees beneath a low cloud while the rain cleared, then through a park next to a grand house with a long line of processional trees, mostly beech, some of them copper, valiant hawthorns; bigger than any I'd seen, a few limes. An ornamental lake to one side.

I walked through Broughton Lees, its triangular green only mildly confusing, through orchards and across slightly dipping fields to a wedding marquee by a church where I almost took a wrong turning. This was Boughton Aluph where a fireplace in the church's porch can be found. The story goes it was for the use of pilgrims waiting to gather in numbers to make their way more safely through the ensuing woods, where bandits were meant to have lurked. The track had turned north now, a sign marking the divergence of the North Downs Way along to two routes; Canterbury for me of course but Dover for others. The valley of the river Stour lay to the East with deep blue and green wooded hills. An A-road down by the river was distant and silent from here.

Godmersham Park was down there somewhere, home of Jane Austen's brother Edward. Edward had been adopted by the childless Thomas and Catherine Knight after they met him at the Austen family home while on their honeymoon. Edward subsequently inherited the entirety of the family estates and changed his surname to Knight. His sister Jane was a frequent visitor and the place is said to have been the inspiration for Mansfield Park. Could I see her in my mind's eye with the library to herself, looking out on a vista of empty tables and chairs and a collection of more than 1,000 books, observing for a moment such a humorous and meticulous observer of the manners of her day?

Then it was up a short climb and into King's Wood. Before I entered, I looked back through a gap in the hedge, over the view to the south; gentle and rolling and wooded. A sign said ten miles to Canterbury. The woods were full of bracken and ash and beech with large swathes of chestnut removed for coppice, the regrowth bushy-looking and almost tropical.

Eventually, after one or two uncertain turnings, I came across a laminated board stating that this was the first place you could see the cathedral (or had been able to before the recent tree growth) some seven and a half miles away. I tried trekking out into the adjacent field for a better view but couldn't see much more. The board detailed an annual pilgrimage from St Martin-in-the-Fields in London which apparently covered some seventy-four miles in four days. People have been making this sponsored walk for some thirty years now, raising money for The Connection at St Martin's and their work for London's homeless. Many of the pilgrims are homeless themselves, doubtless keen to give back and help out the capital's rough sleepers who need physical help as well as prayers, a role that has always been integral to the Church.

The way rambled down to a little, half-wooded road dotted with houses and into the village of Chilham. The parkland of another estate loomed on my left through iron rails, soon to be hidden from view by a high and red-bricked wall. I went in the Woolpack Inn, the first pub I saw, slightly amazed to find it open and waited at the bar for a coffee with a minor sense of triumph. The interior was dusky and heavy with panelised wood. A silenced and subtitled wide screen TV announced Greece's proposed exit from the EU before moving on to reports of the humid uncomfortable nights here.

I left the place by the front entrance and walked up a stunningly beautiful timber-framed street to a small square where I found The White Horse pub and an ancient gift shop full of pleasant tat. Through large gates stood a red-bricked Tudor palace and, in a little enclave, the statues of two pilgrims carved in oak gave the place an added feel of charged sanctity. I felt a mounting excitement with the knowledge that I'd actually get to Canterbury that day. Complex-sounding peals of bells rang from the church.

I walked past the flinty building itself presently, looked through glass doors to see an old couple swathed in the light of stained glass and didn't want to intrude. They, and the scene, spoke of faithfulness in the face of dwindling congregations. Today, people are often quick to mock things which they do not understand and perhaps a simple faith has been harder to understand for many than so many other apparent certainties the world appears to offer. But it sits there as a quiet bedrock still to those who know it, not necessarily allied to the expectation of particular immediate results, but knowing still that somewhere down the line and in some form, every prayer is heard. And the attitude of prayer, as much as any result, can help us to cultivate grace and perhaps be that much more ready when answers and gifts are presented.

Soon I was over a field and along lanes into orchards with half-grown apples like quinces or small plums, smallish trees in row after row of plantations. Fruit pickers were gathered in a mini shanti-town of dark-green portacabins, some slightly battered-looking coaches decking nearby verges to transport them wherever they were needed. Huge, industrial-proportioned crates were stacked for the apples-to-be.

Before an underpass below a railway I met a party of middle-aged women who sounded Dutch or German and who'd started out from Dover. They were friendly enough but somehow their treatment of me was a little unsettling and I found myself welling up with an unexpected contrition; all the things in my life I'd done wrong, the mishaps and betrayals, the times when I had missed my mark, misjudgements, bouts of indulgence or stupidity or pride; they all played on my conscience like never before, habitually pushed away but surfacing now, compounded and immediate and raw. The urge to repent had arisen as if impelled by some kind of outside force. It was all I could do to respond just as well as I could and I spent much of the ensuing miles making silent and personal prayers, all of them given new life.

As if the path itself had suddenly become purgatorial I found myself passing through the long, suburban-like main road of the next village with its copious 'thirties red bricks. Past a couple of rectangular-rooved oast houses, suddenly incongruous, I found myself in 'No Man's Orchard' and sat for some lunch under a mature apple tree. And that's where it happened. A realisation, simple yet extraordinary, not easy but also essential, that I had to find it in me to forgive myself, however unlikely that sounded, however challenging it may be for me to do so.

We're so often told we should love one another when sometimes the hardest thing one can do is to love and forgive yourself. As C.S. Lewis has elaborated in 'Mere Christianity', hating a person is not the same as hating their deeds. We can hate our own misdeeds precisely because we want to love ourselves and those misdeeds remind we are capable of things that go against our vision of ourselves. But we can forgive the man and not all of his actions. We can 'hate the sin but not the sinner' as the saying goes. We are told we must forgive in order to be forgiven and that God loves us despite what we may have done. Not because of any self-image we choose to regard ourselves with or wish others to see ourselves with but because we are part of creation, were made in an image of perfection and in striving for it might one day become a little closer to that state;

another aspect of the vigilance that Chesterton espoused. Just as we may wish that some of our enemies did not do what they have done, we can still wish good for them, hope that one day they become better people. We can only wish the same towards ourselves. In the orchard that summer afternoon, I immediately felt a sense of restoration, like a part of me that had been lost, almost without my knowing, had suddenly been redeemed. There was a sense of treasure suddenly released, a gift that had been waiting all this time, like a laugh from the meadow and trees.

Several years later as I passed through, the orchard was covered in cardboard poppies and poetry tied to the trees, commemorating lives lost, distant relatives, the psychological scars of the survivors. It was the hundredth year since the end of the First World War and churches along the route had been similarly decorated, the path to the porch outside one of them hung with giant poppies knitted from red and black wool. It seemed that almost everywhere you looked that summer there were mementos, ubiquitous metal silhouettes of soldiers with their rifles and tin hats. The war cost the lives of some nine million soldiers with thirteen million civilian deaths directly attributed to the conflict. Every family it seems has a story of somebody lost. Do we ever really question enough the mentalities that gave rise to such destruction? Are our efforts to account for the causes of the war ever really adequate when faced with such loss? Is our vigilance to avert a recurrence on any scale as keen as we all ought to make it? Is it ever enough to remember? In No Man's Orchard the memories of the fallen were borne up by the flowers and words, an expression, when all is said, of the power of an overriding love.

A sign or board just after that welcomed people to the North Downs Way with a drawing of all the places from here to Winchester I'd passed through. It was a sign too, if ever there was one, of an imminent journey's end. Another Dutch-sounding couple came along and we chatted gracefully for a time. They seemed slightly scandalised when I told them I'd been camping out but nonetheless it felt an auspicious encounter.

Just as Winchester was partially positioned so as to make use of the ports of the Wight, Canterbury, Belloc argues, owes its location due to both its equidistance to a variety of ports around the Kentish coast and the freshwater of the Stour upon which it sits. If a traveller or merchant was unsure about which port he would land at or embark from, given the vagaries of the Channel tides, the centrality of Canterbury provided a point of certainty in which to meet fellow travellers or traders. And given that the Stour was navigable to just below the city but that the founders doubtless wanted to make the most of its supply of drinking water, its location made sense from the start.

After a few more orchards, I passed the site of Bigbury Camp, a hillfort allegedly the site of Julius Caesar's first battle on British soil. Given this was the precursor to the city, and thereby the kernel of local resistance, it's hardly surprising the general made a beeline for the place, just as Augustine was bound to head for the later city upon arriving, thereby establishing its tenure as the root of Christianity in the country and the 'knot of South Eastern England', as Belloc has it. The fort was 'the most certain and ancient thing of all that antiquity which had been the meaning of the road... History and the prehistoric met at this point early.'

Belloc liked to write about the primal things; 'the camp, the refuge, the sentinels in the dark, the hearth...', the road being 'the least obvious but most important'. It is, 'for the mass... silent... the humblest and most subtle, but... the

207

greatest and the most original of the spells which we inherit from the earliest pioneers of our race.' In all likelihood our earliest ancestors were nomadic so perhaps we shouldn't be too surprised that that urge still remains. Writing on medieval travellers, Oliver Rackham cites that travel was once seen as more of an end in itself before the rise of passenger-carrying vehicles and public transport. It was the incipient popularity of faster means of transport, the curricles, gigs, carriages, phaetons, drays victorias, flys, waggons, traps and stage coaches, as antiquarians remind us, that began to change our attitudes, including the arrival of the mindset that time spent travelling was wasted. Travel was once a state of existence, not an inconvenient necessity. For all our innovations, the subsequent change is a hard trend to buck. But we can at least quantify the value of the speed and means. Perhaps we need to aspire a little more to slowing right down as our natural pace, with high speed travel more of an infrequent treat, our sojourns for longer, less often.

As Chesterton has it, in contrast to medieval times, these days we tend to see life as a race. Medieval morality, he writes, was replete with the notion that things must balance one another, any movement round a central point 'perpetually altering the attitudes but perpetually preserving the balance', like children encircling a mulberry bush. Today the dancers seek to regain a lost balance by a flight towards an object, 'an object which they do not yet possess'. The established centre of medieval movement was 'rhythmic and recurrent' ours 'precipitate or progressive', very literally of our modern progress, because our goal is unknown. The medieval precursor to progress was order, but it was that of a dance.

I continued on as the track snaked around the base of the fort, its slopes and banks punctuated with stubs of newly cut bushes and trees, mature trees still standing, sentinel.

Then I was finally into the outskirts of Canterbury. The path almost doubled back north alongside a railway or road and a black and white cat sat in a gap in the hedge looking out at the orchard or maybe at me with a sense of calm reverence as if it was silently pleased.

+ + +

In the summer, with the revolt continuing in France and King William of Scotland attacking from the north, Henry decided to go on pilgrimage proper, no doubt in a desperate bid to allay the aggrieved spirit of his old friend. Henry by all accounts was not a religious man. But he may have been superstitious, up to a point. He was certainly conscious of the need for a king to be seen to be pious, a propaganda tool if ever there was one. But, in choosing this pilgrimage now he must have been concerned with much more than his image. He was bargaining for a change in his fortunes, under duress. On the seventh of July 1174 he set sail for Southampton from Barfleur.

While his route was uncertain, the records catch up with him here at what was once the village and leper hospital of Harbledown. Here he dismounted, donned clothes suitable for a penitent; a woollen smock some say, a hair-shirt under a green smock according to others and walked to the chapel of St Dunstan's and the city walls. Chaucer's pilgrims travelling down Watling Street would also have joined our route at this point. Harbledown in The Canterbury Tales was referred to as 'Bob-Up-and-Down', probably a local nickname connected with some home-grown joke but speaking too of the rolls and hollows upon the land around here. The 'Tales' are an unfinished work of course; we never see Chaucer's pilgrims arrive in the city. We leave them in

209

the suburbs here where, as today, to quote GKC once again; 'sectarians and journalists and jerry-builders between them decided that every man should live in the same villa and every man in a different universe.'

As Chesterton pointed out, the Prioress, the Parson and the Knight may have had their airs and could have spent their time in endless fine talk on the road to the Cathedral but they were bound to the Reeve and the Millar by more than just convenience or comradeship. They were bound by something that made medieval religious life more than a feeling or individualised intuition; they were bound by a shared bedrock of belief that had no doubt of St Thomas's sanctity or of the miracles attributed to him and, perhaps more than this, struck medieval society through with a sense of mutual purpose it can be hard to find today. Chaucer reminds us how an incongruous company was bound together by such a purpose. The Summoner and Friar may have argued but their common ground was still stronger. But modern equivalents of the Miller and the Reeve would very likely not have a religion at all. And what would have happened, Chesterton wondered, if the pilgrims followed more individualist urges, if the Prioress had diverted to a vegetarian hostel on the hills of Westerham, or the Knight, disgusted by pacifists, had gone straight to reinforce the fortifications at Dover? It's a better world to not be bound by dogma but pilgrimage at least still offers something that can seem rare today; a shared goal, a fellowship, a sense of unity that overcomes divergence.

Henry made his way on foot through the city, barefoot, cutting his feet on the stones. Once inside the cathedral he was met at the Altar of the Sword Point in the Martyrdom by the Prior and 'Shedding tears… he prostrated himself on the ground, and with the utmost humility entreated pardon.' The great chronicler Gerald of Wales in 'The Instruction of Princes' records;

"The king took off his cloak, and thrust his head and shoulders into one of the openings of St Thomas's tomb… Then he was flogged, first five strokes of the whip from each of the prelates present and then three lashes from each of the eighty monks. When he had been disciplined and by atonement was reconciled to God, he withdrew his head from the tomb and sat down on the dirty ground with no carpet or cushion under him and he sang psalms and prayers all night without getting up for any bodily need."

Henry's contemporaries were astonished and convinced of his sincerity. Was he doing more than going through the motions? And could subjecting yourself, as king, to such a physically painful ordeal have been anything other than honouring more than just the spirit of repentance? Time and events would surely tell. An old monk of Canterbury was reported to dream "Hast thou not seen to-day a marvellous miracle of royal humility? Know that the result of those events which are passing around him will shortly declare how much his royal humility had pleased the King of Kings."

+ + +

As I walked into the city from Harbledown; along the concrete track as it doubled around and then down a Victorian suburb towards a dual carriageway, the heat gave way to a light but sensuous rain. The air remained warm and it felt it could thunder. I'd arrived.

I continued on a main road till the golden-grey stone square of Bell Harry Tower of the cathedral was finally to be seen looming up over the houses. I walked past a steakhouse, past various B & B's where I almost made enquiries but thought better of it for lack of funds. I turned a corner to see a huge stone medieval gate to the city centre, a shiver of excitement and satisfaction running through me. I walked through the gateway by a sideway for pedestrians, gave money to a beggar and then made my way down the crowded pedestrian street decked with its shopfronts and many ancient-looking pubs, enveloped in a miasma of bustle and old buildings. The rain in the heat was just gorgeous, the air and the light thick and mesmeric. A traveller in a doorway asked me for a light, looked me in the eye with a sense of unspoken importance.

A tiny sidestreet led to the towering gateway of the cathedral precinct, covered in scaffolding and sacking now though that didn't detract from its grandness. Foreign students thronged in the narrow road outside. I made my way past and was in, staring up at the pinnacle-ed main towers, the rows of stone saints, clergy and theologians, attempting to take in the grandness of the building and its grey-white stone. Perhaps because it was a Sunday, and to my consternation, the Cathedral was closed to general visitors but a sign said all were welcome to join in with worship. Feeling like I was in at the deep end but with turning back obviously not an option I made my way up along the side of the building to a smaller doorway. The bells were calling to prayer and I joined a small stream of respectably-clad folks as I entered, not a little apprehensive.

I left my rucksack and staff propped up on a pillar and headed into the choir stalls, an elderly man in a suit directing me to a seat and giving me a card for the evensong. The choir itself came in five minutes later, the lower old stalls full of folks while I sat in a modern plywood seat close to

212

the high altar. I took in the stout pillars of the quire, the arches and high windows and elaborate stained glass as the singing began, exhausted and emotional in the best possible sense.

With the service done, I went to leave but had to ask a black-robed cleric of some kind to get access through a now-closed grill to where I'd left my bag. This led me to reveal, not particularly intentionally, I'd been on pilgrimage at which the cleric said I should wait and disappeared into the depths of the cathedral. Presently a female pastor in a black cassock and with greying hair appeared who had a palpable air of utter soundness. She came right up, intent, shook my hand and told me I'd made it.

The pastor led me down to the crypt where a solitary large white candle was burning in the darkness and she quickly lit more so that now the place seemed a little more welcoming. The outlines of stone arches revealed themselves out of the gloom. As we stood infront of the altar, alone in the already-closed building, she said a beautiful improvised prayer for my travels and this pilgrimage, saying she hoped this would be a springboard for me before leading the Our Father. We paused in silent reverence. Nothing I could say at that moment could possibly do justice to all this. To be stood with an ordained woman here in this underground chamber, this holiest place in the warm glow of the candles and spacious, homely dark felt like a grand destination, a suitable end to a journey protracted by years.

She showed me the Antony Gormley sculpture of Becket; a figure made from nails retrieved from the medieval roof during restoration. It is suspended over the site of Becket's first tomb, stark and ethereal, the nails jutting out almost like barbs but also forming a human figure that is graceful and speaks strangely of peace. Becket had attained a kind of victory in death. He had suffered tribulation, persecution and ultimately paid the highest price for his convictions. He certainly had not shied away from death when it had come. T.S. Eliot in 'Murder in the Cathedral' has him facing final temptations; renewed enmity with the king based on false foundations, of the glory and power of a return to political life, to join with those who plotted against Henry. But his greatest temptation, expressed by the Fourth Tempter, was that of the glory of martyrdom itself. Did he conceive himself of a Saint? Had he somehow sought the martyrdom? We can seek to do good but can inadvertently pride ourselves on the action. We can seek to become great, even in self-denial, and thereby fall into a greater snare. Or, as Eliot puts it in Becket's response to his tempters:

"Now is my way clear, now is the meaning plain;

Temptation shall not come in this kind again.

The last temptation is the greatest treason :

To do the right deed for the wrong reason."

The playwright reminds us, as far as Becket's story goes, that it's a little off beam to console and inform ourselves by seeking what might always be an unknowable historical fact. For all the apparent ambiguity, Becket still laid down his life. His faith was sincere. He can only have been aware of the pitfalls that accompany any higher aspiration. We only have a few short hours on the earth. We can only ever strive to do our best. Becket reminds us of our possibilities, our potential as we each of us seek to do better, as we seek to serve a greater peace. Perhaps that's the best legacy that anyone can leave.

The pastor led me upstairs again to an official office with a massive wooden desk and shelves upon shelves that might have been packed through with scrolls, though books were a little more likely; it was hard to take it all in. I later realised it was quite likely to have been a map table, used to help plan pilgrimages to and from the place; pilgrimages to Winchester, to Glastonbury, the Via de Francigena itself to St Peter's Square in Rome. She filled in a yellow pilgrimage certificate and we chatted a little about my journey and pilgrimage in general. She'd done the Santiago de Compostella and I knew that was next now for me. Outside in the nave, three young clergymen in the ubiquitous cassocks were waiting with my rucksack, as if it might pounce at any moment. I appreciated their sense of orderly boundaries. The pastor shook my hand and said "God Bless" as I left and I could only express my gratitude.

It would have to wait for another time to see more of the city and I took a replacement bus home, the last of the day. I sat at the front of the empty top deck as the driver blasted out John Lennon and Elvis, the green lanes of Kent rolling past at great speed. It was for me now to go forward, knowing only everything in my life had been made perfectly new. The summer-clad trees, silver and green in the evening light, parted before us. I knew I was just starting out.

Epilogue

Henry was woken in the night by a messenger several days later in London. Had William of Scotland arrived in Richmond, he wondered aloud? Had Newcastle-on-Tyne been taken? Had his barons been deposed from their lands? He begged the messenger to tell him the truth. But the news was that William the Lion had been captured in Alnwick in a surprise attack. He had been at breakfast when his attackers killed his horse which fell on top of him, trapping him and forcing his surrender. The messenger had travelled four days without stop to bring him the news. Henry was said to have wept with relief. "God be thanked for it," he said, "...and St Thomas the martyr and all the saints of God!"

He mopped up resistance in England, accepting the submission of rebels at Northampton, then travelled to France where his foes flew before him. A peace was secured with Louis at the end of September, the Treaty of Montlouis formally spelling the end of the rebellion. The general consensus was that if the rebellion had been a product of God's wrath, Henry's pilgrimage had now engendered divine grace. Henry was magnanimous to his former enemies and his sons Richard and Geoffrey did him homage (he refused this from the young Henry on the grounds his son was already an anointed king).

For a time, the peace held before his sons, embittered at their mother's continuing captivity, their resentment stoked by Louis' icily manipulative son Philip, broke out into rebellion again, even falling to fighting one another. Henry the Young was confused and caught between two poles; he would ignore his father then plead with him to trust him,

216

crying at his feet. Still frustrated by lack of power, he had jousted to great commendation but remained resentful and turned to Philip. On the outbreak of further war with his father he plundered shrines and churches and soon after contracted dysentery. Repentant on his deathbed, he donned a hair shirt and lay in a bed of ashes with a pillow made of stone. Henry, distrustful, refused his son's desperate request to meet him, albeit sending a bishop instead with the gift of a sapphire ring.

The old king's grief was extreme. With a mutual bitterness not atypical of a classic Norman family, he had paid a high price by not granting his sons more autonomy. He died in misery, heartbroken at the death of the young Henry and ranting at the shock of every one of his sons having betrayed him, the town of his birth having been razed to the ground in the fighting. It all could have been so different. Would he have been up there in historical memory as one of the great kings had he had a better relationship with his sons, or had died earlier, before young Henry rose against him? Some say his promise turned to dust. Some blame it on the fact he never considered himself in the wrong. Some blame it on his pride.

All the same, for a time, his pilgrimage bought him reprieve. He never did go to Outremer, but built memorials to commemorate Becket and sent a small fortune every year in silver marks to the crusader kingdoms. He'd developed the custom of visiting Canterbury on a regular basis and Thomas' growing cult was even appropriated to be associated with the glory of the Angevin house.

The choir of Canterbury Cathedral burnt down in 1174. Upon the completion of the rebuild in 1220, Thomas's remains were moved to a new marble tomb with some 33,000 pilgrims visiting during a festival that lasted a fortnight. It has been estimated that Thomas brought in a third of the cathedral's income after his death. By 1221 this had risen to two thirds. In the Sixteenth Century the Venetian ambassador, somewhat abashed, took in a shrine "entirely covered with plates of pure gold. But the gold is scarcely visible beneath a profusion of gems, including sapphires, diamonds, rubies and emeralds... exquisite designs have been carved all over it and immense gems worked intricately into the patterns."

It was all swept away in the Reformation of course. Henry VIII appropriated a ruby known as 'the Regale' from the shrine, a gift from Louis when the French king visited after Thomas's death to seek divine help with the health of his son Philip, Henry's nemesis to be. The Tudor king took the ruby after the shrine was destroyed, wearing it on his index finger. Though he ordered Becket's bones to be burnt, the story is the monks gave over another set of bones and hid Becket's somewhere in the cathedral or its precincts, their location unknown to this day.

Did Belloc find what he was looking for upon arrival? On the very anniversary of the martyrdom he found the north transept, the scene of the murder, quite cold. He thought to hear some intimation, some echo of the deed but only felt "an emptiness so utter, not even ghosts can return." Was Belloc petulant, exhausted from his winter journey? Had he hit the city on a bad day? Or have our churches and cathedrals become shells, echoes of a former order, peopled by tourists, the curious, the sceptical and unbelieving? It's not hard to feel so sometimes as the crowds shuffle back and forth, determined to get a good shot, to scoop a little history and heritage, a digitised experience to take away.

Whatever our spiritual make-up, whatever systems we pronounce or eschew or cling to bloodymindedly or from the bedrock of belief, it seems one of the best things anyone can do is to remember how to pray. And walking for me is the best way of praying I know. Structure and structures can help with all this and this old cathedral is just one such structure, generations of devotion carved out in a still-living stone. Cathedrals still people my dreams; vast and impossible-seeming at times, built of straw or packed earth like African temples, of golden stone or coloured glass and always lit up. The monoliths of religion stand there as a choice if we feel moved to make it. But for all the reforms, reformations, counter-reformations, the sweeping away of religion itself in some quarters, sanctity itself can never die.

Ultimately all the theories, the doctrines, come down to one thing; the presence of love in the world. We can find that still in these old institutions when we blow off the dust. We can find it in each other's hearts, in dedication to our still-breathing biosphere, in service, in a bond with mankind. We can find it in the face of a beggar given a cloak, in a king's love for a son he would have sooner seen beat him than beaten by death, in a man who chose to face death so as to not be cowed by a friend he'd come to see as a tyrant. Perhaps, ultimately, we can find it in another man who chose death in order to redeem our sins.

Belloc found something of it in an inn of the city where a woman "of a dark and vigorous kind danced with an amazing vivacity." And as much as we may concern ourselves with Heaven this living earth holds a sanctity too, not to seduce us or blind us but as our home, as our very mother just as surely as we have another home beyond the clouds. For too long we have closed the door on her – only by honouring this earth can we truly honour the gifts that are granted with each passing day.

One time, I dreamt of the Goddess. I was in the back of a van in a field. Army or government men, engineers, were nearby, attending to some kind of infrastructure. An old woman, black-haired, stooped, and in ragged clothing, some kind of gypsy, was doing the rounds of their vehicles, begging for something; a little food, a little water. As my turn came, I found myself swept with emotion, gave her the little I had. Something then suddenly shifted. I noticed the rings on her fingers; elaborate, silver and gold and I knew that this woman was some kind of Queen, that we all depended upon her, that we had to look after her in this, her time of great need. Perhaps it's incipient upon those of all creeds to remember this mother of ours, to remember the healers, for so long oppressed, to atone for the long list of wrongs. We need a greater respect for the traditions, not gone, that can help inform what are in the greater scheme of things relatively modern beliefs, to build them back into our articles of faith.

I'd return to Canterbury on other occasions along the old road, my journeys less fraught, more straight forward, rewarding. The last time, I thought about Becket as I walked in the bright summer sun, as if he was somehow present with me on the track. I'd drop into the crypt, light a candle, feel a peace I hadn't felt for years, a real sense of the potency of prayer. Before I left I bought a little bronze coin of Becket as a memento, a medieval image of him from a stained glass window imprinted upon it, replete with a mitre that looked like a helm. I keep the coin in a little pocket of my wallet still and frequently check on it to turn it the right way up, in the hope he can help to make peace with the world, in the hope we can set it to rights.

BIBLIOGRAPHY

PILGRIMAGE AND WALKING

Chaucer, Geoffrey. (1957) *The Canterbury Tales,* translated by Nevill Coghill (Penguin Books).

Cousineau, Phil. (1999) *The Art of Pilgrimage: The Seeker's Guide to Making Travel Sacred* (Element Books).

Hayward, Guy and Mayhew-Smith, Nick. (2020) *Britain's Pilgrim Places* (Lifestyle Press and the British Pilgrimage Trust).

Solnit, Rebecca, (2002) *Wanderlust: A History of Walking* (Verso).

Stanford, Peter. (2021) *Pilgrimage: Journeys of Meaning* (Thames and Hudson).

Ure, John. (2006) *Pilgrimage, The Great Adventure of the Middle Ages* (Constable).

Welch, Sally (2009) *Making a Pilgrimage* (Lion Hudson)

Wells, Emma, J. (2016) *Pilgrim Routes of the British Isles* (Robert Hale).

THE PILGRIMS' WAY

Belloc, Hilaire. (1943) *The Old Road* (Constable and Co.).

Bright, Derek. (2011) *The Pilgrims' Way: Fact and Fiction of an Ancient Trackway* (The History Press).

Cartwright, Julia. (2013) *The Pilgrims' Way: From Winchester to Canterbury* (Book on Demand Ltd).

Du Bouley, Shirley. (1997) *The Road to Canterbury: A Modern Pilgrimage* (HarperCollins).

Hatts, Leigh. (2017) *Walking the Pilgrims' Way: to Canterbury from Winchester and London* (Cicerone).

Jennet, Sean. (1971) *The Pilgrims' Way: from Winchester to Canterbury* (Cassell & Company).

Martin, Christopher. (1999) *The Pilgrims' Way: from Winchester to Canterbury* (The Canterbury Press, Norwich)

BECKET AND HENRY

Eliot, T.S. (1974) *Murder in the Cathedral* (Faber and Faber Ltd.).

Gold, Claudia. (2019) *King of the North Wind: the Life of Henry II in Five Acts* (William Collins).

Goldman, James. (1966) *The Lion in Winter* (Samuel French).

Guy, John. (2013) *Thomas Becket: Warrior, Priest, Rebel, Victim: A 900-Year-Old Story Retold* (Penguin Books).

Jones, Dan. (2013) *The Plantagenets: The Kings Who Made England* (William Collins).

RELIGION & SPIRITUALITY

Arnold, Johann C. (2013) *Seeking Peace: Notes and Conversations Along the Way* (Plough Publishing House).

Aslan, Reza. (2018) *God: A Human History of Religion* (Transworld Publishers).

Carr-Gomm, Philip. (1997) *The Druid Way* (Element Books).

Carr-Gomm, Philip. (2006) *What Do Druids Believe?* (Granta Publications).

Carr-Gomm, Philip. (2019) *Seek Teachings Everywhere: Combining Druid Spirituality with Other Traditions* (The Oak Tree Press).

Grov, Stanislav M.D. and Grov, Christina (eds.) (1989) *Spiritual Emergency: When Personal Transformation Becomes a Crisis* (Tarcher/Putman).

Guite, Malcolm. (2006) *What Do Christians Believe?* (Granta Publications).

Holloway, Richard. (2017) *A Little History of Religion* (Yale University Press).

Lewis, C.S. (2012) *Mere Christianity* (Collins).

Nicholson, Reynold A. (1989) *The Mystics of Islam* (Penguin Akana).

Palmer, Martin. (2002) *The Sacred History of Britain: Landscape, myth and power: The forces that have shaped Britain's spirituality* (Judy Piatkus).

Townsend, Reverend Mark. (2012) *Jesus through Pagan Eyes: Bridging Neopagan Perspectives with a Progressive Vision of Christ* (Llewellyn Publications).

Williams, Rowan. (2014) *Being Christian: Baptism, Bible, Eucharist, Prayer* (Society for Promoting Christian Knowledge).

Williams, Rowan. (2016) *Being Disciples: Essential of the Christian Life* (Society for Promoting Christian Knowledge).

HISTORY

Asbridge, Thomas. (2012) *The Crusades: The War for the Holy Land* (Simon & Schuster).

Chesterton, G.K. (2019) *The Ballad of the White Horse* (Dover Publications Inc.).

"   "   (1932) *Chaucer* (Faber & Faber Ltd.).

Horspool, David. (2014) *Alfred the Great* (Amberly Publishing).

Seward, Desmond. (2003) *The Hundred Years War* (Constable & Robinson Ltd.).

Tyeman, Christopher. (2005) *The Crusades: A Very Short Introduction* (Oxford University Press).

West, Richard. (2000) *Chaucer 1340-1400: The Life and Times of the First English Poet* (Constable & Robinson Ltd).

Wood, Michael. (2006) *In Search of the Dark Ages* (BBC Books).

LANDSCAPE

Cox, R. Hippisley. (1914) *The Green Roads of England* (Methuen).

Hudson, W.H. (2016) *A Shepherd's Life* (Penguin Classics).

Jeffries, Richard (2011) *Wildlife in a Southern County* (Little Toller Books).

Rackham, Oliver. (2000) *The History of the Countryside: The classic history of Britain's landscape, flora and fauna* (Phoenix).